Creative Writing Heals
Volume 3

A new collection from Converge writers
at York St John University 2020

Creative Writing Heals: Volume 3
First published in 2020
by Writing Tree Press

For information contact:
Writing Tree Press, Unit 10773, PO Box 4336
Manchester, M61 0BW
www.writingtree.co.uk

Dedication

The best communities survive the worst of times.
This is for you, Converge Community. Heal well.

In Memory of Philip Gilbert

A gentle soul, a creative writer and a dedicated Converge student who will be missed and remembered with affection by many of the Converge family.

Contents

Foreword

In March 2020 Converge Creative Writing students were just starting to work on their pieces for this anthology.

Then something extraordinary happened. The world turned upside down – but they kept writing.

The global pandemic has been a challenge for so many of us, and it would have been understandable if our students felt unable to continue their studies or their pieces in such a strange and worrying time. But instead, the Creative Writing team found them determined to finish their courses and finish their work for the anthology. We worked online, by email, by post and the now-ubiquitous Zoom, and as a result Creative Writing Heals 3 is full of rich writing: an observation, an escape and a contemplation.

I have never been more impressed by my students' commitment and passion than I have this year. And as a Converge tutor, that's really saying something.

I'd also like to thank them for bearing with us as we found new ways of teaching, and to my team, who, like our students, responded to the challenge with hope, creativity, determination and sheer hard work.

I hope you find some comfort, inspiration and insight in the pages that follow. Congratulations to all our writers for a truly impressive accomplishment.

Helen Kenwright

December 2020

Under the Sun
Holly

Sunrise

Observing the world
I am still a part of
however lost and displaced.

Every day brings a sunrise
a good morning from the universe
a reminder that time passes
at the same speed
for all of us.

The days bring opportunities
The opportunities bring freedom
The freedom brings choices
as we forge our own paths.

There will be a tomorrow.

The sun will rise again.

Power of nature

the forces of nature
control us
imprison us
with the strength of an army

we fight with the elements
storms and snow
heatwaves and hailstones
every condition a battle

each night
the light is captured
darkness conquers the day
our only light from the stars.

24 hours

how can we compress
everything
into 24 hours

because
at the end of each day

we
      all
            want
                  more time.

Seasons

Wooden skeletons stood alone
leaves overpowered
dragged from their branches
stolen by the seasons changing.

Spring will soon breathe life again.

Silhouette

Ruth Middleton

I trace the lines of your face as we lie,
Bodies linked, toes, tickling toes.
I listen to your heartbeat. Our breaths merge and
I trace the shape of your small upturned nose.

You smile dreamily, accepting my need to trace again
the curves of your lips.
I close your eyelids, inhale your smell, try to commit
your silhouette to my memory.
I adore your face, sobbing and laughing
Throughout our many shared years.

Accepting and without blame,
You reminded me at supper, that we had met
Unexpectedly today. I'd gone to the butchers,
You had popped out of the office

For a packet of crisps, more likely a sneaky fag,
I know you smoke away from me.
When you saw me on the street you stopped,
Put your hand on my arm, I shook you off.

You didn't speak at first and I looked at you
Unsure, confused, not knowing
But your voice was familiar, its tones, the spacing of
your words
The h's that somehow stick in your throat.

I hope you didn't see my panic
At not recognising you.

I trace the lines of your face,
Pleading with my fingers to imprint
This beautiful, wonderful, loving
Magnificent face into my faulty memory.

Your smile is wistful, you take hold of my finger,
Squeezing my hand you seek to reassure.
Tonight, together, intertwined,
Tomorrow you will once again, be a stranger on the
street.

(Prosopagnosia, face blindness, is increasingly
recognised. In my case, it was one of the disabilities I
acquired following a traumatic head injury.)

Grandma: my heroine!
Audrey

Tall as round
    A ball o' feistiness
never had a chance
    to show off her intelligence

19 year old son drowned off Yugoslavia in t'War
    and husband's TB death seven months later
condemned her to demeaning work to feed her
daughter
    donkey-stoning neighbour's steps for a
ha'penny
        no 'Good Old Days' for her….

Many's t'time we hid behind t'sofa
    "Rent man's here, Keep Quiet!"

Other times she were 'ospitality incarnate -
complete strangers invited in
  open door, sit 'em down, tea and a slice of cake -
    "Na then, who are you?"

But came the day Mum's abusive partner

found us and knocked on t'door

Sweet old lady turned into Bradford Boudica!
frying pan in 'and
she   chased   the   b*****d   down   the
terraced street
and out of our lives for ever!

Yes. Truly.

My Grandma is my HEROINE!

Commuting
Michael Fairclough

You get the bus most of the week to commute to work. Every day the same, get on, get your ticket, and take a seat. Want to get off? Ring the bell, breathe in and squeeze through the masses' morning migration. But today, your choice of distraction fails you as your battery dies or you find you have forgotten the book you told yourself you would finish and so.

You get the bus. You get your ticket and take a seat then at the next stop someone you recognise gets on. Somewhat relieved as they sit next to you, you chat the ride away until they get off and so you turn to look out the window to pass the time until your stop. That evening on your way home, you decide to look out the window again as a stranger sits next to you this time, browsing something on their phone.

The next day you get the bus and take a seat, and realise you are sat on someone's hand. You turn to apologise, seeing yourself in the window and follow your reflection down, you are sat on your own hand after putting your change in your back pocket. You laugh to yourself as you pull your hand free. Getting back on later you scan your ticket and the bus driver winks at you. You begrudgingly wink back and take a seat near the back of the bus.

Maybe Wednesday you get the bus and ask for a day ticket. The bus driver winks at you as they hand you your change, but you're not in the mood and find a seat at the back and just stare at the little camera dome. Pressing the bell to get off, someone walks past you dressed like you, strange you think as you watch them get off ahead of you. Riding back home that evening, you take a seat and notice a baby staring at you. Smiling at the baby, you do a little wave to which the baby winks at you. Not sure if you were seeing things with how deliberate it appeared, you look around then back to the baby, the baby winks again. Getting off the bus to get some fresh air you walk the rest of the way home.

Another day you get the bus and take a seat next to someone. They are brushing their teeth. They must be running late you think, they don't stop and continue to brush their teeth when getting off the bus. That evening you get back on the bus and sit near the middle, an empty bottle rolls beneath the seats and out the open door, you hear a small voice say cheers mate. Looking out the window it's dark already, shocked you blink awake at the end of the line, having missed your stop.

Maybe another Wednesday, you can get the bus on more than one Wednesday you know? You get the bus and on getting your ticket you sit at the back and begin to read the adverts they are all in French, are you French? You think to yourself or is the bus French? Getting off the bus later at the Arc de Triomphe you wonder if you will catch the ferry home.

The next morning you get the bus and take a seat next to a bell, a few stops later someone sits next to you. On pressing the bell at your stop, it lets out a soft moan of pleasure, embarrassed you dash off the bus and head straight home and spend the rest of the day in the shower.

Getting on the next morning still wet, you take a seat near an open window. Glancing down to the frame, you notice a funeral for a dead insect. His gravestone reads, *01/04/2020 – 01/04/2020*, so young you think. That evening you get on, it's standing room only, coming up to a corner the bus bends in the middle lengthways it gives you a headache.

The following day you get on and take a seat. A few stops later someone presses the bell to get off and everyone changes seat. Following suit, you take a seat near the emergency exit, reading the little frame around the mini hammer it says in case of emergency break neck. You hope it's not mandatory.

Getting on that evening you slouch into a seat in the middle of the bus. Tired, you almost doze off and are eager to get home before you fall asleep. Your stop coming up you press the bell and your arm falls off. Staring at it in disbelief about its treachery, your disbelief changes to betrayal as your legs get off without you.

Putting yourself together the next morning to catch the bus, you wait at the stop and as the bus pulls up you get on. The driver turns to look at you and without saying anything he puts his hand up to the dividing pane. Mirroring him you move your hand to his and as you look into each other's eyes you say,

"Father come home, Mother is ill." Shaking his head no, you reside yourself to your previous task and ask for "a return to town please."

Choosing to sit in the middle of the bus due to

used condoms on the back seats, you settle into the ride when all of a sudden they start playing tinny music from their phones, no one says anything.

Maybe a Friday you are running late and get the next bus. It is surprisingly busy just past nine, but you remember bus passes can be used from nine onwards and sit near the back. After a couple of stops, the bus slowly fills up with elderly people and you notice them avoiding the folding seats and at the next stop, a woman would rather stand than sit on them. Curious now, you watch them and after a while you notice a pregnant gentleman going for them, slowly folding one of the three down, he sits and lets a relaxed look cover his face. The seat then proceeds to fold up on the man and swallows him whole.

That night you stay late and in turn get a later bus. On getting on you notice the driver immediately as he smacks a flat palm repeatedly on the dividing window, his features drawn and gaunt, he looks at you with pleading eyes as green smoke slowly fills his partition. You scan your ticket and take a seat. Hearing a dull thud a few stops later you glance up and see the driver collapsed, head against the window, but the bus does not stop moving until the next designated stop.

Tuesday, standing at the bus stop you wonder when things will go back to normal. Noticing the bus coming down the road, you put your arm out and as it slows you move back the mandated two metres away from the doors. The driver can now safely disembark. Once clear, you proceed to pull out your decontamination kit and yellow marigolds and get to work sterilizing the driver's seat.

Pulling up at your destination, you observe the queue of potential passengers is quite long, spaced evenly down the pavement and around the corner. Going to open the door, you stop shocked, the next person in line is spaced 1.6 metres away from the doors at most. Refusing to open up you set off again shaking your head in disappointment as the man is pelted with loose change.

Sometime later you get the bus, glad things are back to normal. Taking the only free seat you sit down blindly only to land on the floor. Looking around confused you discover the whole interior is just painted on, getting off you examine the bus closely. It's just a big cardboard box, trying to act casual you wander off down an alley.

After cleaning your clothes of wet paint, you try again that dinnertime. On getting the bus this time however you're suspicious so sniff everything for paint fumes, even Norris on his way to Bingo. Taking a seat, you move a copy of the metro only to find someone has placed a landmine down. It being the only seat you debate risking it, what's the worst that can happen? You think to yourself you were going to the pub to get legless anyhow.

Easter weekend you get the bus at your leisure, taking a seat you watch people get on and off and again you notice the person dressed the same as you. The back of their head mocking you, you hate them, you don't know them, but you know you hate them. Staring the back of their head down as they get off the bus you notice they begin to run immediately on getting off.

That evening, halfway home a ticket inspector gets on and begins to work his way down the bus, overly eager you get yours out before he makes it past the first row. And on getting to you, you hand him your ticket. Plucking it from your hand with finger and thumb he snorts a laugh of derision upon inspecting it and claims, "I've had better," before handing it back.

A new week you get the bus and take a seat over the wheel arch, the speed bumps jolting you, making sure you don't nod off. Dazedly looking down the bus you watch as the door opens at the next stop as the person from the other day gets on. Clearly winded from running, they scan their ticket and make their way to where you're sat and proceed to sit on your hand.

"I hate you," you say to yourself.

"Well maybe you should spend less time in your head?" you reply.

"But you're all I have; I need to entertain myself somehow."

"I know, I think I'm just tired of talking to myself is all."

"Me too," you say.

Love is an Eternal Masterpiece
Charley Perryn

'When love is at the base of something it is a masterpiece. '

Steve Maraboli, *Life the Truth and Being Free*

This poem was written in response to the above quote that I chose randomly in the first session when we discussed what a masterpiece was.

Love is eternal.
Love transcends time and space,
Love transforms into formlessness Beingness.
In Beingness we expand our consciousness
And we perceive the formlessness of love.
We realise we are never alone
As we are Home.

From that place of feeling at Home, springs a belief in myself that I am an artist and anything is possible. I have spent a term of exploring what a masterpiece means to me and I found something truly magical. I wrote the following poem in response to this insight.

The Greatest Masterpiece of All

Within each of us is an artist
Waiting to be released.
It's part of human nature to create.
We can draw, sing, paint and act,
But because of lack of opportunity
Some of us believe we could never do that!
Or we try and give up.
It's not good enough
Or it doesn't adhere to
The establishments idea of how
Art has to be.

The true masterpiece is not the end product
But the creative journey itself.
Beyond the mundane,
There is a journey into freedom,
Into the realm of imagination
Into Beingness itself
And in that place magic happens.

We rise above the humdrum
And see possibilities that we
never thought existed.
And change then happens through us
Not to us.
Our mind and heart becomes open
As we flow with the creative freedom
 To a destination of our own choosing,
Not some dictated notion
Of how we thought it had to be.

We may find incredible art
Hung in a gallery or sculpture park,
But perhaps the greatest masterpiece of all
Is when we look in the mirror,
    Smile, and see the true artists we are!

My Little Brother

Esther Clare Griffiths

'Wake up darling.' Mum gently stoked my head. Tugged from deep sleep, my mind still awash with fog-thick dreams. Why were the skylights black? My little brother coughing again, long rasping wheezes, pulling me awake, a soundtrack to my dreams. Longing to go back to sleep, I began to drift. Mum took my hand.

'Come on love. We're taking Jesse to the hospital. We need to get his cough checked.'

Ushered to the door, our cottage a whirl of leaving, I pushed my feet like lumps of clumsy iron into clunky brown shoes. I kicked them on, a rush of resentment - not for being dragged from dreams, but for my shoes. I imagined my feet in elegant, pointy heels, clickety-clack, clackety-click, so grown up. Instead I was stuck with sensible, heavy ones with thick pale brown laces, ready to trip me. The colour of poorly poo. I wanted to shred them into a million little pieces.

Black plastic car seats slapped cold and stuck against my skin still sleepy warm. Usually Jesse and I would laugh at the sound of our skin unsticking, but not that night. Dad drove into the darkness, pitch black, like a cloak thrown over my head. Still those hideous fawn laces shone back at me, lurid in the pitch black. I leant into my seatbelt as our dark country lanes twisted and turned, lurching one way then another. Jesse sat on Mum's knee rasping and coughing, and in the gaps a tight still quiet, just the buzz of our Renault 4 and the cold gleam of the blue light. I liked asking Dad for the blue light, every primrose bank suddenly illuminated white. Not tonight. My breathing caught in my throat, fast and shallow, quicker than Jesse's rasps and wheezes.

My eyes flashed with sudden hospital lights, cold, harsh. Blinking and half running, I kept up with Mum. Dad held Jesse locked tight in his arms. We raced down long corridors, weaving through nurses, stark strip lights, bleach, bustle and noise. I gripped Mum's hand hard feeling the urgency. 'Bring him in here.' A Doctor in white showed us a tiny room. Dad lay Jesse gently, quickly onto the bed, propping him up with starchy pillows. I stood near his feet watching his face pallid, almost silver grey, like moonlight. Tubes ran in lines from his mouth, plastic, clear - drinking straws without the curly bends. I stood quiet, staring at my little brother, holding my breath, shoes forgotten. Dad leant over Jesse, muttering under his breath, his face red in the hospital heat. Older kids in pyjamas ran down the corridor jumping on trolleys, racing, shouting and laughing. My eyes glued to a night nurse as she swept around Jesse's bed, a tide of smiles in the loud bright chaos, dark hair spilling from her pale blue hat. A matching dress too. I made up my mind right then and there to be a nurse. I will be just like her. She carried a child's plastic seat in one hand, the colour of a powder blue spring sky and placed it by the bed. Dad and I left Mum half asleep upright in the tiny chair. Jesse's bed stretched way past his feet, two little bumps under a snowy waste.

I held Dad's hand tight when we returned next morning. We found Jesse quiet and still, lost in his white wasteland. Mum crumpled from hours on the hard, blue chair, and the trolleys, kids - and worst of all, the night nurse gone. Instead an unsmiling nurse clipped in and out, all in white, crisp and stark, like the constant sharp lights. With his eyes closed my little brother looked dead. My throat clammed up, a sore and tight lump of tears. I loved him so much I wanted to cry. Mum reached out tired arms and I stumbled onto her lap. Jesse's hair lay half stuck to the pillow - always a messy fuzz of tangles, as yellow as the hay bales we were always jumping from. His face was peaceful. I stared hard and saw a tiny rise and fall of the snowbound sheets. I reached out and touched his little brown hand, all scrunched up in the bright white folds. Still holding on. Still with me.

Henry O
James Richmond

1.

They walked through the fields, through the mud to the dirt track where the bus would pick them up. A fine grey rain filtered down upon them making the mood sombre. This trip would be to England and then to America on the Titanic. An escape from humble farming origins to carve out a new more prosperous existence in a new world to venture to new horizons aboard a new giant wonder ship.

The child Henry O Flaherty and his family travelled hopefully seeking out
a wonderland, a place where their minds would find a new serenity, the placid lake of happiness, a new contentment where they could live full rich lives free from the dense bog of humdrum familiarity and grey dull existence. How better than to travel aboard the latest state of the art giant ocean liner. It seemed only beauty and cool enjoyment of life lay ahead.

Alas things rapidly became very cool indeed but not in the manner they had wished for .
As the ship jarred to a halt in the dead of night the image of the pot of gold at the end of the rainbow and the whole concept of peace of mind began to evaporate like an ice cube placed on a hot stove .

2.

The old giant clock ticked the sixtieth second and its large hand creaked and jammed into place. Another hour. As Dylan Thomas once wrote Time has ticked a heaven round the stars.

After his parents' death in the Titanic disaster Henry had been adopted from a New York orphanage at the age of 15 by one of the richest families in America. The infertile couple were seeking an heir to their fortunes.

Their one condition with the uneducated Henry was that he transform himself from lowly farm hand to educated aesthete and also attempt to seek some meaning to life by virtually spending all his time in their vast library in their stately mansion house.

Below the giant clock Henry had been pouring over Darwin's theory of
Evolution. The more he read the more he began to ponder the meaning of existence. It seemed one could make plans and put in one's best efforts for the whole thing to be wrecked in an instant. One could build for a better life for ages only for it all to be
ruined in no time. Equally a hapless ne'er-do-well could instantly be elevated to hero or millionaire through mere chance.

Onc constant seemed to be that all human life was finite. Time was utterly reliable. What one did in time was one's own choice. One's own conscious awareness of time would end. This was called by humanity "death" and it was almost universally feared and disliked.

3.

Henry also observed from his studies that despite this extreme hate and dislike of death
humanity had been fighting and slaughtering each other for centuries consistently.

Over arguments about how people ought to behave or use this time they were given. One particular prophet who surfaced and advised people not to do this got
nailed up to a cross to by the humans who then went on to use his arguments as
further basis for why they should persecute and hate each other.

These realisations began to weigh heavy on Henry's mind.
The sheer stress of the "answers" he unearthed seemed to distort his understanding
Of what was honest truth and what was illusion. Or like a mirage in the desert.
A kind of hallucinatory promised land where the answer to what life really was about or meant would emerge then slip like sand through the fingers where all reason seemed blurred or rendered meaningless.

He began to hear voices ordering him to disrupt the will of fate that had lead him to be charged with seeking meaning to existence by deliberately acting as

if there was no point to life other than hedonistic excess. Henry had moved unbeknownst to him
into the arena of the mind where silence was the same as violent noise and everything seemed utterly ridiculous utterly hilarious and was flooded with exploding manic distortion where right and wrong or a conscious awareness of the real or unreal was no longer possible or cared about and total chaos become the format of time.

When did time start or end? No one knew. Nothing seemed to matter.

4.

As it was the jazz age Henry O got into jazz at the parties. This music became the meaning of life to him. He went to jazz gigs in New York. He heard the great Charlie Parker play the new modern jazz music known as bebop. This inspired him to take up the saxophone himself. Over the next few years, he spent his time practising sax in the library instead of looking for meaning in books.

He became after ten years a highly proficient jazz musician.

Through playing he would forget all the problems of this world and feel transported to another world. He found an agent and they moved back to Ireland where they toured the country playing the music. He became known as the man who'd survived extreme adversity and brought beautiful music to people who would then through the music
forget about the meaning of life or its worries.

Artistic freedom of expression had been brought back to them from the new world.

They loved him.

Money

Philip Gilbert

My brain is strained by
bills to pay
always another one
in the way.

I will get into trouble
if I don't give them
all my money.

To them I'm just another number
a statistic in their book.
Spare change for the homeless guy
I wish I did have money to give away.

I just play the lottery
£2.50 a go
Some hope
I must me mad
To think it would go my way.

© Philip Gilbert 2016

This poem was originally published on the Converge website, and is reproduced here in celebration of Philip's life and writing. He is much missed from the Converge Creative Writing community.

For the Love of Poppies
Caroline

She couldn't remember when she first started to like the deep red poppies. It was highly unlikely that it would have been from the garden at home. Her dad was a landscape gardener, so anything that dared to grow, did so in straight, regimented lines. Weeds were exterminated without mercy!

Perhaps that is where her love of nature began. The soft flow of grasses and higity pigity appearance of delicate plants, growing despite being neglected. Her belief that 'a weed is just a plant in the wrong place' was her attempt at rebellion, even if she would not dare say it to anyone in the family.

She remembered with sadness the beautiful flowers in full bloom, Dad pulled out of the ground, because it was time the next season's scheme was planted. Bright colours replaced by tiny plants surrounded by the bare soil, who, in most probability, would never reach their full potential. She remembered the beautiful tulips and daffodils languishing in straight lines on the patio. Drying, her dad said, to let the goodness go back into the bulb for next year's show.

Not one flower was cut and brought into the house to be admired. They lay like uprooted ruined jewels, sighing when the wind blew, in an eerie lament.

Neither did she think her fascination came from the plastic poppies Mum and Dad bought every year, in November, to remember the glorious heroes. She wasn't sure who these heroes were. She was mesmerised by the fact that beautiful fields of blood red poppies had grown where people had died and were buried as a result of war. She thought of the poppy as a release of a soul and vividly displaying the futility of war. As she grew older and the wars continued, she mourned for the lost souls, who had given their lives for their families and countries.

She wondered if you put a red poppy where someone had died as a result of war, or at the hand of another, would our Earth become a red planet?

She guessed there would be some parts of the Yorkshire Dales and Moors, Dartmoor and Wales that would still be green. Maybe you would need to go back to the War of the Roses, or even 1066, to get a true reflection.

In biblical terms, even in the first family, there had been a murder with Cain and Abel. Perhaps humans just had an inbuilt compulsion.

Throughout her life, she wondered why the human race didn't learn from history. Was human life so cheap, mere cannon fodder. Does killing a rival, or having a gun or fighting for another person's property, give a person extra importance?

Are we a creation born to mourn? It is the one certainty in life, that we will all die. We just don't know the time or day.

Yet despite this, she still loved poppies. To her it

seemed a sign of hope, seeing a delicate red poppy springing up in a piece of wasteland or roadside verge. One of her fondest memories, was seeing a field of poppies on holiday in France. Photos just didn't do it justice.

Her first expensive treat to herself had been a hardback version of the *Diary of an Edwardian Lady*, new, not even from a charity shop. How she loved the sketches in that book and longed to be able to draw. Her home was filled with poppies: on curtains, pictures, crockery and artificial flowers. No-one was in doubt about her fascination with the poppy!

She had tried and tried to grow poppies in her own garden. It was overgrown and ramshackle but she was sure they would grow easily. She'd collected seed and read up every suggestion of how to cultivate. But somehow they never did.

But then, she had never let her true nature loose. It wasn't war or envy. She didn't use a gun. She was sure no-one would really miss that busy body Mrs Hynd Richards.

Just as she hoped, the following year she had the most abundant show of beautiful red poppies. Later, she read, there was still no lead in the strange disappearance of her neighbour.

She

Heather

Eddie was a hard working fisherman, who loved his job. He was a happy bloke who was loved by all who knew him. The fact that he was 6'4", broad shouldered with a deep voice and rough hands from working hard didn't detract from the warm hearted, easy going nature and gentle spirit that he had. He was a loving family man until his wife and child were killed in a road accident, then he poured himself into his work. It was six years ago they were taken away from him; he grieved in private and loved nothing more than having a good laugh while he worked.

He expected a lot from those he worked with, but he was fair, and worked just as hard, if not harder some days. On those days, he would tell them all to, "Clear off!" "'Aven't you lo' gor 'omes t' go t'?" He'd shout. A good strong Yorkshire man, born 'n' bred on't' coast, he would often clean down the boat and finish off some of the things that needed doing and send the guys home early. He'd always bring a flask of tea and some sarnies but hardly ever even looked at them while he was working, and would always have it just before leaving.

One day, a normal day just like any other until the boat comes into the harbour, the crew are busy looking over to the shore, then Eddie spots her in the distance. A woman on the cliff. His heart races and he feels an overwhelming sense of responsibility for her - he couldn't believe he may be about to watch someone jump to their death! This time it was the crew who told Eddie to leave early. He ran out of there like his shirttails were on fire, jumped in his car and went over the speed limit all the way till he could see her. He pulled over to try and ease her away from the edge. What should he say to stop her jumping?

She was there still near the cliff edge, the cold icy wind blowing all around her; she was mostly oblivious to the traffic behind her, but the slamming of a car door got her attention. She looked over her shoulder to see Eddie walking towards her, very slowly, with a strange look on his face; his arms outstretched in front of him, palms down. That made her wonder if he had done something wrong.

They spoke for a while, and Eddie was relieved to know that she had no intention of jumping. They shared his supper together, talking and looking out into the waves sparkling in the moonlight. A new friendship formed that day, from someone getting the wrong idea, seeing something and thinking the worst, then running with it -- to laughing over how different the reasons for her being on the cliff were.

2 Poems

Mary C Palmer

It's okay to be alone
Watching the rise
And setting of the sun

To stand alone
The only one
Safe n sound
With both feet
On the ground

I listen to
Radio two
To hear a voice
Coming through

Songs I love to hear
Sometimes
I dance like
There's no one here

Just me
Just by myself
Just being me.

~*~

Time just keeps
coming and a going

Is there heaven
Is that where I'm going

Afraid to close my eyes
Afraid to sleep
So Afraid to close my eyes
So Afraid to sleep

If you're there dear Lord
Please hold my hand
For only you can hold me now
Don't let me leave this wonderland

Help me make it through this night
Give me the strength I need to fight

It's 6 o clock
Is it morning
Or is it still the night
Don't know where I'm going
I can't bare the fright

Please hold my hand Lord
Help me through this night.
For only you can hold me now.

The Dust Bowl

Amy Stewart

We call it the Dust Bowl.

The place where the sea was, but isn't anymore. Now, it brims with things long dead: fish bones sticking up out of the dirt, crab shells, hollow and freckled with dust like burnt-out motor homes. At the very edge is a thin slip of water, widening out to somewhere further away.

Soon, the school will move again. We can never hack away enough distance. We advance on the tide, and it retreats like prey. No one knows why. My parents are out there somewhere, beneath that strip of water. Trying to find out why in the last seven years, our oceans have dried up to a surface area smaller than England.

The winds are always hot now. Hot as bath water. A breath of it licks across my face, gritty. I'm not supposed to be out here while everyone is still in their bunks. First thing in the morning, the teachers come out to clear the debris left by another sucking away of the sea. Whatever's taking the water, it's killing the animals too. The teachers scoop up the bigger carcasses before we come out for morning rec. They think it's too traumatic for us to watch, but how could we not? It is the only part of our day with any variance. We peer out of the single portacabin classroom, but we treat the occasion with the solemnity it deserves. No one speaks. No chatter, no questions.

One morning about a month ago, there was a whale; its torso empty and open like the ribs of a cathedral. Some of the flesh was still on the bones, scraggly bunting strung across the middle. It took all the teachers – and that's four, including the caretaker – hours to chop away at the whale and remove it. I can still see it, if I close my eyes.

There's nothing new out here this morning. The wind howls across the barren space, stirring up dust in the deep places. I've seen pictures of reefs, in books. Electric purple and pineapple yellow. The book said people used to go diving for pleasure. The water would surround them, and they'd just… float, like butterflies with masks. It makes me thirsty thinking about it, makes my limbs buzz with weightlessness.

I take a step forward.

It wasn't a conscious decision, to travel across the Dust Bowl, to chase the water on foot. I don't really believe that I'll find my parents when I reach the sea. That I'll reach the sea at all. But there's only so much sitting, waiting and looking at pictures in books that someone can do before they reach out to try and touch something real.

My first problem is the sharp slope where the sea wall gives way, revealed by last night's tidal retreat. It's an almost vertical drop of about twenty feet. The school has all kinds of machinery and equipment for this very purpose: diggers to excavate, levellers to correct nature's work, great big 4x4s to keep us moving. But my departure would be far too obvious if I stole one of those (and somehow figured out how to drive it). I have no option but to get down onto my hands and shuffle down. I barely hesitate. It surprises me, this boldness, after months of inertia. Before long, my slide becomes a tumble. The rough earth grates my elbows and dust sticks to the back of my throat, but at least I'm at the bottom, looking back up at the school framed by a cloudless sky. It is ugly in the way that only purely functional things can be. Three portacabins: one for sleeping, one for eating, and one for learning. Twenty of us all together, four staff and sixteen children, kids of absent scientists. I never want to see it again.

I brush myself off and stand up. The glimmer of water on the horizon appears to have moved backwards already. As the sun shines down, shrill in its heat, I start to walk.

If you were to ask, most people would tell you that the world's waters simply evaporated. The oceans started disappearing as the earth got warmer, so it's a natural conclusion. I'd forgive the wider world for believing that, but at the school, we know better. We have scientists for parents, after all. Heat doesn't explain the shrivelled creatures left in the wake of the tide, who look as though something has feasted on them from the inside out. Our parents left to prove the theory that whatever was sucking the oceans dry, it was coming from beneath the seabed. We watched them leave, six months ago now, their sub slipping beneath the surface like an unconscious body. It's dizzying, to watch something sink and not come back up. You feel like you've let something die.

There are, of course, the religious zealots who see

something biblical in the state of things. They view the dry, cracked earth as a punishment. And then there are the conspiracy theorists, who think it was the Russians, and need no further logic. Everyone's got their theories, and they love to shout about them online to anyone who'll listen. But as far as I know, no one is actually doing anything about the oceans but our parents. *My* parents.

"There's never just one reason for anything," Dad told me the night before they left. "Things are never as simple as they look. There are a hundred forces at work on any one thing, at any given time. Remember that."

I have. Remembered that. As the days ticked by and our parents didn't come back after the allotted three months, someone (it barely matters who) floated the idea that they never would. I put that idea in a small box, somewhere deep and dark, and vowed never to open it while there was still a chance. There are a hundred different reasons my parents could still be alive.

Equally, there are a hundred reasons they could be dead.

In my latest development session with Ms Krunk (we have these in lieu of parents' evenings, there being no parents to attend), she told me I'm quite clever, but reckless. That I'm a big picture person who becomes frustrated with detail. I had never thought these things about myself, and I feel that, actually, it was quite reckless of *her* to plant the ideas in my head, because they seem to have become a self-fulfilling prophecy. I am crossing the Dust Bowl, with only a single bottle of water and an out-of-date protein bar. I wonder if Ms Krunk will get any kind of satisfaction from knowing she was right.

The sea doesn't seem to be getting any closer, though there's dust caked all up my legs now, making them chalky and dead-looking. The topography arches, bucks then surrenders under my feet, and I have the general impression that I'm travelling down, down, down. My ears ache. My knees burn. We've learned about the abyssal plains in class – great stretches of flat earth covered in sediment, thousands of metres below surface level. I imagine this is where I'm heading. That this is where the last of the sea, the slice of weak light in the distance, is pooling now.

I don't have the same passion for science that my parents did. Do. It's an intrinsic part of their relationship to life, how they make sense of the world and their place within it. They are both curious, erudite, and almost monk-like in their dedication to *finding things out.* Our classroom has at least three of the books they've co-published. My parents look out stoically from the back flap, Dad with his frothy lick of grey hair and Mum, her pale eyes intimidating even in 2D.

I've always preferred words, though I'm mathematical about them. Precise. Not a writer, but a collector. I like combing the dictionary for spiky, uneven ones, storing them away in my memory. Counting the syllables in poems and haikus, understanding how and why the rhyme works. I like studying technique and effect. Mum always thought

I'd come around to the sciences, but Dad seemed pretty happy, unsurprised, about my predilections.

"You'll be one of those people who thinks of new words for things," he told me once, before he started the ocean project and we started living at the school. "Is there a name for that?"

There is. A Lexicographer. To me, the word is undulating yet harsh, its shape unpredictable, like waves in a storm.

The sun is high above me now. I must have been walking for three hours, four. Blisters are pulsing under my thin socks, but at least the water is getting closer. Close enough that I can kid myself I smell salt, seaweed. If I really, really concentrate, I can bring to mind the skittering caw of seagulls. But I can also hear engines, their low, mechanic chant. The school will have sent out 4x4s to find me by now. Looking back over my shoulder, I see only miles of dust, rippling in the heat, but I know they're there. I need to hurry.

The other kids at the school range in age between 11 and 16. I'm the oldest. Perhaps for that reason, or because it's my parents who led the expedition, they ask me constant questions. When will our parents be home? Where has the sea gone? How long will we have to keep moving for?

I give them answers, the best ones I can give. But I want answers too. Calm words come out of my mouth but in my head I'm screaming.

I don't know,
I don't know,

I don't know.

The 4x4 is gaining on me now that I'm close to the water. It'll be a matter of minutes before they haul me back to those nearly-white portacabins, hastily erected over and over again. I won't get into any trouble for running away, nothing more than a stern word. I'll just return to the same half-hearted lessons, the wondering, the looking out of the window, and that is somehow so much worse.

I break into a run. It's so hot that I feel my scalp crisping. Something squelches in my shoes each time my heel makes impact – sweat, or maybe blood. But I'm so close now.

I was just going to put my toes in, but when I get to the glistening shore, I feel the water lap my ankles and I keep running, for a full minute or two, until I'm waist deep. I breathe hard, fingers trailing, floating. I close my eyes. It doesn't smell like salt, or seaweed, or anything like that. It smells sour. The water isn't cold, but warm. It shouldn't be this warm. What could survive in here?

Behind me, the 4x4 comes to a stop. I hear doors open, close, my name being called. It's almost time to go. My eyelids flutter open and I peer at the horizon for the last time. Imagine my parents under the surface. Pray that they're still down there, somewhere, that they've somehow survived what's killing everything else.

And that's when I see it.

A tail, breaching the water. Flat and ready as an open palm, dual fins hitting the water with a mighty slap. I watch the space it touched long after the tail disappears.

A whale.

I actually whisper it to myself – *whale* - my mouth widening and contracting, breathing life into the word. I hadn't thought there were any left, had thought the waters too shallow and poisonous now. But there was no mistaking that tail, the enormous might of it.

I let my mind run through its trembling tornado of thoughts. What if the oceans are filling back up? What if the worst is over? My parents – they could be down there. They could have figured it out.

They could be coming back.

It is quivering and fragile, this hope, but kindled now. A fierce flame, where before, there was only ash. That hope stays with me as I willingly climb into the 4x4. It cradles me as we crawl our way back across the Dust Bowl, and back to our days of waiting.

The Long Goodbye
Brenda Hodgson

Two doves on a rooftop,
Signifying Peace and Love,
As we said goodbye to you,
You've found your freedom at last.

Sleeping so peacefully,
Late in the day,
God was releasing you
From the pain of MND.

You were one of the heroes,
Working as a medic,
A life of selfless service,
All you did was much to your credit.

The times I'll remember
Will be happy and free,
When we were laughing about past times.
All the things we found so funny.

Facing adversity,
You found the courage to live,
Kind and courageous,
You had so much to give.

I'll always look back,
Missing your voice,
The Christmas dinners we shared,
The cakes and fruit crumbles that everyone loved.

Of course we had low points,
When I let all of you down,
As I faced my own illness,
Or just wasn't around.

But when we got over the
Bad times again,
We were there to support you,
And see you right with holidays we shared.

Whenever I hear the soft call
Of a happy wood-pigeon,
It takes me right back
To that beautiful garden.

Enjoying the sunshine,
And a fresh cup of tea,
As we shared good times together;
It was all meant to be.

Entwined Hearts

Junior Mark Cryle

Long ago, in the age of magic, a time of peace and prosperity was shared amongst the many races across the land.

Elves mingled with Dwarves, Men feasted with Goblins, Griffins flew with Pixies. But the most unique co-habitation could be found within a magnificent valley, between the forest-dwelling Dragons who occupied the land for centuries, and the water bound Mermaids that entered through hidden underwater tunnels. While no animosity was between them, they rarely interacted with the other except on passing. Mermaids were known for their lack of interest in matters on land, while Dragons were unsure if the water dwellers were food or not. Thus the two races kept to themselves, having lived by a silent pact: Leave it be and be treated likewise.

Until a chance encounter between two younglings, who wandered from their families, changed the status quo; one being a yellow-eyed Green Dragon hatchling called Duragon, a Western breed that, in their youth, resembled winged reptilian puppies with big bubbly innocent eyes; the second a grey-eyed violet-haired Mermaid hatchling named Melody, human in appearance except for a fishtail where legs would be, otherwise she resembled a mortal baby in the early years.

Melody was submerged like a duck at the time as she searched for shells, her silvery-blue tail flailed in the air which caught the hungry Duragon's attention, who bit on it without hesitation.

Both yelped in surprise, one in pain, one in confusion, none in fear.

Recovered from the initial shock, the two soon interacted as younglings would, both drawn together by their curious fascinations, both stayed together for the company they mutually enjoyed.

Sometime later their parents, worried for their offsprings' safety, found them having fun and without disturbing them, began to interact with each other.

Over time they drew the attention of their respective friends and families, which inevitably led both sides to revise the silent pact; to share knowledge and traditions in order to benefit and assist the other. Thus it came to be that future interactions were encouraged and, in time, became a natural aspect of their lives.

Years have passed, the two grew into majestic beings in their own right.

Duragon, though small compared to his brethren, became a formidable beast.

His bumps and nails grew into sharp claws and two mighty horns, with spikes on his snout and along his spine, eyes narrowed and harsh yet remained innocent, hair-like growths lined his chin as it were a beard, broad leathery wings, bladed tip on the tail, all signs of a grand creature.

Additionally, he favoured a bipedal posture despite being quadrupedal in nature, yet was agile in the air and swift amongst the trees, his fire burned in blue flames instead of the world-renowned red, a rare yet promising trait in dragons to indicate untold potential.

Melody herself grew and developed into an elegant form. Her skin pale yet healthy, tail prismatic and fins that glittered whether under sun or starlight, beauty enhanced by her peachy lips and ruddy cheeks, and a melodious voice that mermaids are known for. But what stood out the most were her short vibrant hairstyle and piercing pearly gaze, uncommon for mermaids as long hair and alluring eyes were the norm, yet served to enhance her radiance whilst having concealed a studious and meticulous mind.

Gone were the days of childish games and juvenile antics, through their time together they became more than they believed by learning from one another.

Melody taught the young Dragon to swim, strategize, use his smaller size as an advantage, and conserve stamina in dire situations. In turn, Duragon taught the fair lady stealth tactics, cloud reading and sound recognition to judge potential threats or prey, at which point she chose to shorten her hair to avoid reduced visibility.

Their respective lessons came to the test when it was time to enter their respective adulthoods, one of the many traditions that Dragons and Mermaids shared in celebration for those who passed of course.

For Dragons, they'd compete and search the valley for treasures to build the biggest hoard possible within a cycle of the sun, as a Dragon's hoard is a sign of respect and wisdom, only then would they be recognised as Adults.

For Mermaids, only those who could sing with melodious harmony, enough to make even the ocean itself respond to it, would be seen as true sirens of the sea.

First was the Dragons' trial, with selected mermaids to assist if violence broke out.

As most of them took to the sky in search of potential riches, Duragon opted for an underwater approach. For he learned from his time with Melody that great treasures could be found from sunken ships of old, far along the ocean's bottom, the pressure from which held no threat to him courtesy of the diamond-hard scales that protect his reptilian hide. It was thanks to such insight that Duragon was able to pass the trial, in the shortest time compared to past trials.

Next was the Mermaids' trial, with selected Dragons on standby if acquired. Through the underwater tunnel to the ocean the mermaids took turns to sing for the attention of the sea creatures, those who attracted the most would pass.

Before Melody could take her turn, the creatures broke into a violent frenzy, as the more carnivorous ones snapped at the gentler beings.

Before any dragon could intervene, Melody started her song, for she noticed whenever she would sing around Duragon and his brethren they would become relaxed and content. She later discovered her potential as her voice would often stop Duragon and others from fighting rough with just a few musical bars. While she never practiced such abilities on anyone beyond Duragon and two other dragons at most, even she found herself at awe as not only were the sea creatures calmed, but also compelled to dance around Melody in time with her song.

Unorthodox as it was, to ignore such a feat would dishonour traditions, and so Melody too had surpassed expectations and was awarded as such.

Both had been accepted as full-fledged adults, an achievement that both were thankful to the other for.

Despite the increased differences in appearance and longevity, Duragon and Melody continued their interactions, sharing each other's experiences through swimming and flying. The more time they spent together, the closer they became, until they reached the stage that being without the other left an empty feeling that neither could explain.

Then came the fateful day that peace ended, and war began. With some races able to get along and encounter minor issues to overcome, others found it troublesome and often fell out over any issue, as is the case with Dwarfs and Elves, for they often fight for resources for their respective crafts. Such disputes would involve whatever allies they had at the time, forest natives such as Centaurs and Wood Nymphs would side with the Elves, whilst mountain dwellers like the Trolls and Rock Golems aided the Dwarves, with more who shared the animosity or had their own agendas, noble or otherwise, that would have joined eventually. And the more participants in a civil war, the more divided and hazardous the world would become.

The Dragons and Mermaids, despite offers from other races, opted to stay neutral in such conflicts, only willing to fight in order to protect each other and the livelihood they had grown to cherish, in the valley they called home. To ensure this, the dragons took routine aerial patrols across the outskirts, whilst the Mermaids sealed the underwater tunnels with guards on rotation.

Months had passed, and it was a day off duty for the two friends, who intended to make the most of it. Before their agreed meeting, Duragon woke up early that morning to pick out the ripest fruit he could find, and Melody arrived at their usual place just as early, to find the best flower to put in her hair to be as presentable as possible, given that their time together had been few and far between.

It was during this time that a hunting party consisting of five human-sized Orcs, accompanied by twenty boar-sized Goblins and three Ogres as large as Elephants, arrived covertly at the valley, their natural colours blended within the green foliage to avoid the dragons' attention.

Armed with various light tools, including short and mid to long-range weapons, and adorned in thick leather armour, they approached their destination: the lake where Melody sat on the water's edge humming to herself, unaware of the danger that laid in wait.

The hunters identified the objective; their employer informed them of tales regarding

Mermaids, notably those that say one could gain immortality once mermaid flesh is consumed.

As they took their positions one of the goblin's steps broke some twigs, the snap caused Melody to stop mid-hum, as her sessions with Duragon taught her what the sound indicated and, given their meet-up wasn't due yet, knew it wasn't him.

She made the jump to dive for the safety of the water, only to be yanked back to the shore with enough force to wind her, a sense of pain drew her attention to the cause; a spear with a line attached had impaled itself near her tail's base. Then she found herself ensnared by a fishing net before she could attempt to remove the spear, the hunting party moved in to ensure their catch couldn't escape. Melody was able to let out a single cry for help before she was gagged and pinned to the ground, pushed for time an orc prepared to carve out her heart, as a live mermaid would only slow their escape. The job description of "Dead or Alive" allowed hunters such on the spot flexibility.

Trapped and helpless, she found her thoughts turned to that of Duragon; her heart fell to despair at knowing they would never meet again. As the Orc was about to strike, a familiar roar drew the hunters' attention moments before they were scattered like leaves in the wind, the netted mermaid saw her saviour landed and towered protectively over her: Duragon!

Being near enough to hear her cry from before, he abandoned the fruit he diligently picked and flew to her aid without hesitation, but upon the sight of

Melody, any relief of her safety was replaced by an intense rage towards the ones who harmed her.

As the hunters regrouped from his earlier arrival, he charged in flight to break them up again, but as he flew past them one of the Ogres snatched his tail in his grasp before he threw the dragon back to the ground, hard. The pain from the impact brought some sense back to Duragon, along with awareness of his immobilized wings, greatly damaged as they took the brunt of the fall, which left him only one option.

As the Hunters moved once more towards their quarry, blue flames came forth to separate the two, the fire burned intensely as if beckoning a single fool to attempt passage, only to be burnt alive as a reward.

With a furious roar, Duragon made the challenge: they'd claim the mermaid over his dead body!

The gauntlet thrown, the hunters accepted the challenge, the fight had begun.

Claws clashed with blades, flames flicked on armour, arrows bounced off scales, maces smashed with tail. Hunter vs hunted, invader vs invaded.

A swipe of a claw knocked back the Goblins, a swing of the tail toppled the Orcs, both of which gave the reptilian beast a chance to toss one ogre around with his fangs and horns before the cycle repeated.

As the hunters reduced in numbers Duragon dwindled in strength, only his primal rage fuelled his assault. In what rational thoughts he retained Duragon's strategy was firmly set in his mind. He would hold them back until the other dragons see the battle from above and join the fray, or the Mermaids resurface to aid in Melody's escape, yet he took personal satisfaction that until then he'd make them pay for their acts with their lives. A moment few dragons would experience and, as long as Melody was safe, he would relish it until the end.

All the while Melody spent that time to escape the net and remove the spear from her tail and used the still lit flames to heat the spear's edge enough to seal her wound, much to her discomfort.

The act, along with her absence from water, drained the strength Melody needed to flee. As the battle waged she waited with bated breath, having fought all temptations to jump into the fray, lest she would endanger herself and her battle-worn protector.

Reduced to only three Orcs, the Hunters fought on. All who heard of Dragons knew they were one of, if not the, most formidable creatures in recorded history, with enough strength to crush armies. But as with all creatures strength had limits and whether Duragon was aware or not, he was tired. The tired make mistakes, mistakes become costly.

That was when the tide of battle turned; an Orc took the chance and struck Duragon with their secret weapon: a spear forged to slay Dragons. A deadly strike that caused the valiant beast to fall, much to Melody's horror.

As the hunters approached to deliver the final blow, Melody, who could tolerate no more, jumped high and over the flames to land in front of them. She took advantage of their momentary stall to shriek at a pitch high enough that it disorientated them before it rendered them unconscious.

Other Dragons and Mermaids appeared shortly after in response to the noise, the former carried the hunters away for disposal while one aided Melody back to the water, the latter tended to Duragon's wounds.

Melody waited in silent prayer for his life, as the Mermaids used their arts to heal the Dragon as much as possible. It wasn't until night had enveloped the land that they ceased their work, allowing Melody to rest by his side, the only indication that he was still alive was the slow-motion his scaled body made as it moved up and down, indications of his breathing, and slow it was indeed.

Many days passed since then, all who heard of what transpired left the valley be, fearful of the consequences. This reprieve gave time for the recovered Duragon and the thankful Melody to talk long and hard about what happened, how they felt, what they had, and what they almost lost.

It was then that they made the choice, under the next lunar eclipse when magic was at its peak, to accomplish what has never been attempted between different species: a life bonded union.

The two races were unnerved upon the announcement, as such a union had never occurred before, but having owed the two for the life they've cherished they spent the next year in preparation.

The time had arrived. The lunar eclipse, without clouds to obstruct its form, shone with twilight across the valley, the centre of which where the ceremony was located and where the ritual would be held, stood the Mermaids and Dragons closest to Duragon and Melody, who were as ready as they could be.

The Ritual had two aspects; the mermaid part was a passive aspect, for they would become immortal themselves if they bonded with one closest to their heart, an achievement that mermaids strived to achieve; the Dragon aspect, an active one at that, would help identify this.

For if two Dragons fully trusted one another, they would split their hearts in two and exchange one half with the other, an act that would forge a link between them until their lives ended. All the thoughts, pain and strength one experienced would be shared with the other as it were their own.

Magic was not an active power that Dragons possessed, so they would utilise magical power on events such as the eclipse to perform their sacred acts.

While Duragon had his own claws Melody used the spearhead she kept from that night, with Duragon's knowledge, to perform her part. Their hearts were split, the two halves exchanged, then re-joined with each other as if never apart. Before anyone knew, the wounds healed independently before any Mermaid could do so, a sign that Melody, and by extension Duragon, had gained immortality. Proof that, with no more doubt, the feelings the two shared were tried and true, for all eternity.

With the rituals completed, as the races cheered in merriment, the two embraced under the light of the moon as the eclipse, and the magic it provided, came to an end.

And so, as the times of the world changed, as loved ones came and left through the years, as each conflict raged and resolved from each generation, Duragon and Melody lived on in the comfort of the bond they had forged.

Centuries have passed, the age of magic long forgotten, the age of science and technology reigned supreme, yet in a corner of the world, away from civilization of any kind, it is said that those who dared to venture into the mysterious valley could see signs that its occupants still remain.

A Dragon and a Mermaid, together in the promise they made long, long ago:

"From here to eternity".

The End

Poems

Keith Myers

1.

I am a postman taking parcels and letters.

Watching out for dogs that may upset us.

As we go up and down each street,

My earphones on, listening to the beat.

If parcels are too big for letterboxes,

Try knocking on doors for someone to take it.

When answered, please could you give it to the recipient.

Moving along we get the bag empty,

We move on to another place,

Same routine, different pace.

My mask and gloves on, I look a right case.

2.

We are at Cordukes 004,

My poetry is inside the door.

1 hour from 1 to 2 o'clock

No time to go to the loo.

A different subject must start each poem so,

When it's began away you go.

Lynn comes feeling not too bad

William is doing a synopsis of his work,

Clare is writing back to front in her large book

Ned Kelly is the hero she took.

We have not to be disturbed at all,

So do not shout or call.

After the hour is up,

You may drink out of your coffee cup.

As you leave the campus

There is a shush.

St John's you have done us proud,

Let's say it out loud.

3.

My Colin Firth

Has a wonderful girth.

Mr. Darcy is my name,

My life will never be the same.

I am admired by a lady

Who may be quite shady.

Her name is Helen by the way,

His name is mentioned every day.

Helen knows he has many suitors

But she knows who is cuter.

I will play it along for a time

If I see him I will mime,

Come to see me my time fellow,

Colin, Colin, I will bellow.

He moves towards her and says what a nice lady,

I would like to call you Sadie.

Whatever you say says Helen with a smile,

They hug and Colin stays just a while.

They meet up at a later date,

Helen says I must not be late.

They have a picnic and a bottle of wine,

She hopes he will be mine.

They go for a walk

It seems so natural they talk and talk.

Where it will lead I do not know,

But my Colin is a lovely bear.

The wedding we hope will be a grand affair

We will be happy and we will both share.

Lovely times ahead

I will put the tale to bed.

Goodnight.

4.

I am sat in a café

Having a latte and scone, talking to an old friend.

I stroke a black Labrador sitting beside me,

We talk about old times

We have a reminisce.

Let's go outside for a walk,

Take in the scenery and lovely weather

Seeing other people together.

We cannot do that,

Because there is a virus that's worldwide

We are concerned at every side.

Boris says wash your hands regularly

Try not to pass it on,

March and April to get through

Hopefully it will go, and we can carry on my son.

5.

It started on a summer's day,

Sun was shining, everyone at play.

I took my dog for a walk out,

Labrador Mack is taken all about.

Over fields, on pathways, meeting other people and dogs.

Chasing a stick or throwing a ball, he will fetch it back the mog.

After walking several miles,

We sit and have a rest and I sleep like a night on the tiles.

Woken up I have as a cruiser goes by with people on board.

Enjoying the weather as we all carry on as a cord.

Over bridges we walk, nodding and smiling at people passing by,

We do make the effort and try.

Mack and I arrive back. Tinned food for him and a meal for me,

Lets see how we go again on a path near the sea.

6.

I am going to the shop today,

We are open to sell essentials I say I say.

Will you keep two metres apart,

Do not come any nearer to my cart.

What have we got, pies, sandwiches, and sausage rolls,

Then batteries and razor blades, the next aisle calls.

Envelopes, pads, rolls of this and that,

Even DVD's to rake through at the drop of a hat.

We move on to biscuits, coffee and tea,

Tins of soup, crisps and sweets to look and see.

Milk and magazines to come before the checkout,

If no one there, use the self-service machines.

No you shout.

They say start, pass your items through,

Money in, please take your things and go away

phew.

Please mind yourself on way out,

Not too close to others or they will shout.

7.

Let's go for a run,

Look up and see the sun.

Perhaps four miles to loosen up

Let's go over Scarborough Bridge,

There may be a train going by, so wave your cup,

Under the bridge we go and back through again.

Let's skip by the hotel and rail station, no people

to see

Along Blossom Street, and up Taddy Road,

Crossing over, watch out for cars, none about, take cover under a tree.

Drink of water and take the outskirts of the racecourse,

A nice breeze take me round and as I leave the course.

I jog to a finish and check my meter, four and a half miles,

That should set me up for a night on the tiles.

Inside mine, nothing open like the pubs and clubs

So if you fall over it's at your own risk

Straight to sleep, head like a whisk.

8.

The weather is still wild today.

Shall we go out in it I say, I say.

Fallen trees, branches blown everywhere.

Wind is making it more colder,

Leaves and litter blowing off my shoulder.

Headlong into this, my face is red raw,

Too strong for brollies is against the law.

Everything is hiding till the storm dies down

Birds shiver in whatever hiding place they own.

Trains not running

High sided vehicles not going over the Humber Bridge,

People hold on, as cold as a fridge.

The Beans Talk
Karen Wilson

Do they still eat porridge in prison? Jack pondered to himself as he stared out of the window into the near distance, at nothing. He was thinking about Ronnie Barker in that old prison show 'Porridge', wondering if prison was still like that. G would have enjoyed her time in there if they did serve up porridge every day. He had often wanted to ask her throughout their correspondence , but could never bring himself to raise the subject. It was too close to the bone - an impertinent reminder of her offences. He never knew what would upset her or not, so he was especially careful in his letters not to touch on unmentionables or anxiety provoking subjects.

He continued to stare out at the back garden, where the strange new plant was growing rampantly. G would soon be here and they would finally meet after all these months of letter writing. His mother had tactfully left the house for the day, to give them time to get to know each other. This was a demonstration of uncharacteristic sensitivity after the recent weeks of accusations and criticism since her 'bereavement'- which is how she now referred to the loss of their cow, Daisy. But that was another story.

Jack carried on day-dreaming, musing now *Do beans talk?* as he stared at them cooking in the pan on the hob. The way they wiggled over the heat in their thick tomato sauce suggested a form of communication known only to themselves.   His intuition was correct, and as he stared blankly they were, in fact, chatting freely amongst themselves.

Just like Englishmen, they usually conversed about temperature. When they were imprisoned in their tins, stationary on the shelves of a supermarket or domestic cupboard, they were cold and claggy, and moaned about low temperature and close proximity to other beans. One would think they would relish the heat as a welcome contrast when they eventually reached a pan or microwave, but still they moaned. *It's far too hot in here* or *it never used to get this hot* one would state to another as a conversation opener. But at least with the heat came movement - they were all compelled to separate from those they had become closest to, as they were jolted into activity by the sudden heat and swishing of a wooden spoon.

And with each fresh contact came gossip , which was what they loved to do the most…

Today the talk was of Jack himself, and could be heard throughout the pan. *So gullible!* began one, *I'm amazed his mother is still speaking to him. Hardly speaking* replied his companion, *I would say her attitude has been passive aggressive about the whole thing.*   Steering the conversation away from the mother back to Jack, the first bean stated *He's always had his head in the clouds.* Meanwhile, at the outer edges of the pan, the rumour that the family were *HAVING TO GO VEGAN NOW* was just beginning.

The letterbox rattled. Loudly. Twice. Jack was shaken from the world he had drifted away into. G must be one of those people who announced themselves like this, he realised. Most would knock on the door, but some were flap rattlers.

Leaving the beans to their chatter, he dashed from the kitchen and threw open the front door to greet her. He had expected a vision of blonde loveliness but her hair was lank and straggly. Her face was sallow, bruised and scratched- the consequence, it transpired, of a brawl on her last night inside.

As they made stilted small talk in the hall, the focus of the beans' chat now switched to G's arrival and had turned from gossip to a chorus of bitching: *not even a real blonde; always been so fussy about her food; a spoilt, entitled little brat; she made a total mess of that house, even the bedrooms…*

When there came a break in the cacophony one old bean took the chance to regale a small group of acquaintances with the specifics of G's lengthy record - *Breaking and Entering, Damage to Property, and Theft*, he declared, *not to mention the Squatting. I thought squatters had rights*? replied another and there began a heated discussion about the topic.

In the hallway, the heart that has soared all morning is now plummeting. G is not what Jack had expected and he is terrified as he begins to explain the issue with lunch.

He begins by reminding her of what he had told her in his letters about Daisy and the market, then explains that no cow means no milk, which means no porridge. It gradually dawns on G as they come through into the kitchen and Jack is gesturing towards the pan, that he is preparing Beans on Toast, instead of Porridge, for her first meal as a free woman. Her grey pallor turning a deep crimson, she snatches a huge carving knife from its block on the side, then grabs the pan from the hob. She hurls the beans up the walls before dashing across to the back door, pre-empting any thoughts he might have of escape.

The blade glinting in her clutch, Goldie locks the door, then turns on Jack just as he is blacking out.

The Scene of Crime Officers have a hard job distinguishing between the bean juice and the blood of an Englishman when they arrive - the walls and kitchen floor are awash with both, and they have blended. Goldie has fled the scene, as is her modus operandi. Unaware that the beans can talk, it doesn't occur to the Detective Inspector to call them as witnesses.

Which is a shame because they are all desperate to tell someone everything they have seen here today.

Urban Jungle

Angi

too many people
too many vehicles
too much noise
too much stress.

The city is a pressure cooker -
all concrete glass and steel,
modern, almost brutal
patches of sky reflected in glass.

The city is a cage with tower block bars.

All kinds of people -
different creeds and cultures,
social status
scurrying like ants in society's maze.

no time to see
no time to connect
no time to think
no time to just be!

Simply Black

Llykaell Dert-Ethrae

Simply black is the cat
That sits upon the wall
In the light of the moon,
Watching little mice crawl.

Simply black is the hat,
That rests upon her head.
So delicate, so fine,
That's what everyone said.

Simply black is the bat
That flits upon the night,
Beating leathery wings
With its astounding might.

Simply black is the rat
That crawls upon the floor,
Gnawing and nibbling,
Always looking for more.

Simply black is the night
That sets upon the towns
Everyone's asleep now,
With no more tears or frowns.

Self-Fulfilling Prophecy?

Louise Raw

It was late March 1997 when I lost control of myself. I was driving my brother, James, to a cousin's birthday party in Whitby. We were heading over the moors, past Pickering, and it was beginning to snow. Great white flakes hit the windscreen. James was moaning bitterly about the council bungalows at the end of his street, how people on low incomes always cause trouble. I was twenty-seven, two years older than my brother, unemployed and still living with our parents – and so his little tirade grated.

It wasn't until he started talking about Jenny that I really began to lose it. Jenny was a friend. Sometimes, I thought, my only friend. As soon as her name cropped up in our conversation, alarm bells began to ring. Then he said the words that made me snap.

"I got her drunk. Even though she was plastered, she wouldn't let me put the light on. I thought it was because she was a bit chubby, but no. I didn't need to see, I could feel the scar tissue on her arms and legs. Why would anyone do that to themselves?"

There was a sharp drop to the left of the road, where the moor fell away. No one would know, I thought. It would just be a tragic accident. I put my foot on the accelerator and yanked the steering wheel. Then I began to see the past vividly before my eyes.

May 1975

I'm building houses out of cards in my bedroom when James comes in and kicks down the card house, then kicks me in the thigh. I push him away and shout at him. He wails, and my mother rushes up the stairs. She's wearing a green and white polyester dress with a large collar.

"She hurt me, Mummy," he wails at her.

She ruffles his hair and comes for me. She sits on the bed and pulls me over her knee, then whacks me hard on the bottom with the purple, plastic hairbrush in her hand. She hits me again and again and I scream the house down.

"Bad girl, horrible child," she says as she hits me.

I don't know if it's the pain or the unfairness of it all that's making me scream so loud.

July 1977

I look into the kitchen from the doorway. It has fitted cupboards made of a flimsy wood and covered in white plastic. My mum is sitting on a stool, crying. My dad has his arm around her and she leans her head against him.

"What's wrong?" I ask.

"Horrible child, you don't care," she snaps. "Go away."

I turn around, walk into the living room and slump on the fake leather sofa. I hear James come down the stairs and he, too, goes into the kitchen.

"Mummy," he cries.

"Come and give me a hug," she says. "Good boy."

June 1978

Rainbow is on the black and white telly. I'm laying on my belly on the living room floor, transfixed by Zippy – a puppet with a zip for a mouth.

"Diane," my mum says.

"What?" I say, not turning from the television.

"Look at me when I'm speaking to you," she says.

I tear my gaze reluctantly from the screen and look at her.

"A little girl drowned in the river yesterday. You really shouldn't play there."

"It wasn't Maria, was it?"

"No, it wasn't."

"I don't care if it wasn't Maria."

"You want it to be another little girl in your class?" she snaps angrily.

"Noooo," I say and shudder.

"Well, that's what you said. You remind me more of your grandmother every day. She was a cold, cold woman too."

July 1985

Emma comes to call for me, dressed to kill. She's been shopping and is wearing her new clothes: a grey jacket with shoulder pads and a straight silk shift that comes to the middle of her calves. She's far prettier than me anyway, but seeing her all dressed up makes me feel a complete mess. I'm wearing scruffy jeans and a burgundy and white striped acrylic jumper. My hair needs washing.

"Shall we go to the Crown?" she says on the doorstep.

"I've got nothing to wear."

"Come as you are."

"No," I say.

"Don't you ever do anything on impulse?"

"Sometimes, yeah, but I want to watch Live Aid…"

"Suit yourself," she says, and turns and walks down the path.

"I don't blame you, pet," my mum says, hovering behind me in the hall. "I wouldn't have gone either."

I smile tentatively at her and she smiles back.

"Anyway, you don't want to miss Live Aid."

"No," I say.

August 1987

I'm standing in the kitchen doorway again. The cupboards are now pine. My mother is wearing a headscarf over her rollers and is making herself a cup of coffee. News of a man going beserk with a gun is blaring from the radio.

"I would die of shame if you ever did that. To think a child of mine…"

"I haven't. I wouldn't…"

"You remind me of him. He thought he was something special, too."

"I don't."

"You do."

August 1990

I'm sitting in a psychiatrist's office. There's a child's drawing of a cat on the wall. The psychiatrist is a plump woman in her early thirties, wearing bright pink lipstick.

"I'm destroying Romania with my mind," I say. "I can't stop it."

"Do you believe that?" she says.

"Yes, I do."

"Would you like to come into hospital?"

"Yes."

She picks up the phone to book me a bed.

October 1991

I'm sitting behind a till at Marks & Spencer's when James approaches with a beautiful girl I don't know.

"Not her," the girl says. "She doesn't look clean and her eyes don't look right."

"Okay," James says. "That queue there looks the shortest."

They sweep past the end of my till, heading for the short queue three tills over. James averts his eyes, still pretending he doesn't know me. I want to shout at him, shout at her and tell her my acne doesn't make me unclean and what does she mean my eyes don't look right, but I don't. I serve the next customer who approaches politely.

January 1992

A cold, dark winter evening and I let myself into the house, dump my coat and bag and walk into the living room. My dad is sprawled on the chintz sofa and I take a deep breath.

"They didn't renew my contract," I say.

"Can't even make it as a shelf stacker. What good are you?" he snarls.

"Something will turn up."

"You'll never amount to nowt. Get out of my sight."

I do as I'm told and head for my box room.

March 1993

I'm curled up on my single bed in the box room, writing. I'm writing what I think is a ground-breaking novel: a story of walking in other's shoes, virtual reality and crazy psychologists.

I still haven't got a job.

June 1994

I have a job in a call centre, which I hate. The callers often lose their temper with me. I receive rejection after rejection for my novel. My mother and James read it. They are the only ones that do.

September 1996

I'm lying on my single bed again, reading James' published novel. It's my idea, albeit told with considerably more style. I look at the acknowledgements at the back. Mum, Dad and various friends are mentioned, but not me. I seethe inside.

February 1997

It's a cold, wet Tuesday afternoon and a group of us are at the library writing away in a back room. Jenny and I are the only young people there. She laughs her warm laugh after I've finished reading aloud my tall story and I smile at her, smile inside.

*

Then I was back in the car, careering towards the edge of the moor. I heard a voice, half inside and half outside my head.

"You'll be what they always said you were, if you do it," it said.

I yanked the steering wheel again, just in time, and the car veered away from the edge. I steadied it as James clasped his hands to his head and said, "Jesus, Di, have you got a death wish?"

"No," I said, looking at the road ahead. "No, I haven't."

"Are you alright?" he asked.

"Fine, absolutely fine," I said and looked him in the eye for a moment, before turning my attention back to the road.

What a Funny Fluffy Easter Bunny
Christina

This little fluffy bunny is looking rather weird
With its squat little face and cheeky littles ears
Could it be a chipmunk, guinea pig, even
something else?
And where is it hiding its little button tail?
As I sit and ponder this funny looking thing
I want to pick it up and snuggle it under my
chin,
as I sit watching as it hops round the field, it
looks like it's loving nibbling on the grass
Then I settle down to eat the chocolate eggs,
relishing my wonderful little Easter gift.

Expectations
Andy Milne

Air salt odorless in,

Smells for searching

Places in ready eyes with,

Ends backwards with journeys on.

Rest and refuge

Seeking those from hiding

Cloak's own Nature

Of layers in submerged

Shelters wooden invisible

At out look backs aching

Snow crunching on

Feet tired of soles

Untouched mountains of

Tops kissing, skies softening.

Seem they as always not are things

Things are not always as they seem

Softening skies, kissing the tops

Of mountains untouched,

Soles of tired feet,

On crunching snow.

Aching backs, look out at

Invisible wooden shelters,

Submerged in layers of

Nature's own cloak

Hiding from those seeking

refuge and rest.

On journeys with backward ends

With eyes ready in places,

Searching for smells,

In odorless salt air.

Return to the Island

Catherine Dean

[A sequel to Catherine's story in 'Creative Writing Heals:2]

Having completed the Herculean journey from Yorkshire to the Scottish ferry terminal we had a wait of a couple of hours. We finally caught the evening ferry which took another two hours. Our spirits began to lift as we were delighted by the clear view of the setting sun as we approached the pier at Port Isaac. I was a university student, in my early twenties. It was almost ten years since we had been before. Hector had not changed one bit, a little greyer perhaps, but still fit and full of energy. He looked immaculate, wearing mid-blue shirt and pressed trousers. The weather on the rugged island had not taken its toll on him. I remember my paternal grandmother telling us that once he had stayed with her in Liverpool whilst on an accountancy course. He had arrived with a tiny haversack. Before retiring each evening, he had washed his shirt and hung it on a coat hanger to dry so that it was ready to wear the next morning.

Hector had kept us up to date of his news by phoning us annually at New Year, or out of the blue at other times, always in the early hours of the morning. We had not missed out on his colourful life. He regaled us with his sailing exploits to places such as Ireland and Portugal and his travels to Japan and

South Korea. He also told of his latest inventions, business exploits and various relationships.

On that first evening at Hector's lodge he showed us photographs of his son, Hamish who was now three years old and lived with his mother on one of the northern isles. Later Hector began to reveal stories of his epic trips to Tory Island. He was a true raconteur, being half Scots and half Irish and enjoyed scaring us with ghost stories of local ghouls who inhabited the ruins of Kildare Castle. Hector had lit the room with candles and turned off the lights which added to the atmosphere.

We were interrupted by the arrival of Hector's friend Emma and daughter, Laura, who were dropping off some groceries. After Emma had left, he told us that she had been a good platonic friend for years. She had had a relationship with someone from the mainland, but it had not worked out long term. Her daughter was born not long after the friendship ended. Laura was a similar age to Hamish and the pair got on well when they were together on the island.

The next morning, we set out to explore the island in Hector's old Volvo. Hector tooted the horn and waved at every passing car or pedestrian he saw. He explained it was considered rude not to acknowledge other people. Suddenly he stepped on the brake at a remote cottage and jumped out of the car encouraging us to follow him. We found ourselves in a workshop next to the house, which was full of black ceramic objects. My brother was taken by one depicting a monkey sitting on a pile of books, whilst examining a skull – 'Alas poor Yorick!' We bought several souvenir pieces which we still have. The artist himself has since emigrated to Canada. Hector told us he liked to support local craftspeople as it is difficult for them to make a good living on the island.

After a light lunch at a local hostelry, we returned to Hector's house where he suggested we should pay a visit to his trimaran, which was moored in the harbour, as he had to collect some WD 40. He needed it because the lock on his front door had become stiff. 'Let's go out to my boat in the harbour', said Hector, ' I have left something on board.' We agreed that it sounded like a good idea as the weather was so fine and the sea calm.

Hector's boat was moored in the harbour about a mile from the cottage, 'Quartz Haven'. We drove down near the shore. Hidden by some rocks was his wooden rowing boat. Hector said to my 19 year- old brother, Jim, 'Can you row us out to my boat?'

My parents were proud and encouraged him - it was character building! My brother, Jim was delighted, although he had very-limited nautical experience. He had once commandeered a boat for a sail around the harbour of St Ives after all. Jim rowed us out to the boat one at a time. Although twenty years have passed since then, it seems like only yesterday. Eventually we had all reached the boat. It was yellow and red in colour with the distinctive three hulls – hence trimaran. We inspected the facilities onboard. The minute galley kitchen was cluttered with gadgets and other debris. We could see the three mountains from the bay rising majestically into the sky. Hector had climbed or run up them several times.

The sky was an azure shade of blue and the beach and sea were bathed in sunshine. We did not go for a sail that day. The waves were not choppy but there simply wasn't time. We were only there for two days after all. My dad reminisced about when he had been out in the rowing boat on my parents' honeymoon, where he had been petrified that they would get holed on a reef which could be seen in the clear water.

Hector proudly told us about his boat, 'It's called 'Memec' and although it's a little cramped it has everything I need to hand. Up front it has one sleeping berth and two full sized berths in the middle section. To help with navigation there is a small navigation table which has a GPS plotter and radio for weather forecasts and for communicating with other boats or harbourmasters prior to port entry.'

I told him that I thought it was a lovely structure, I said, 'I am envious of you.' I had no nautical experience except for pedal boats in Roundhay Park, Leeds. Usually it was me being rowed about.

Hector continued to tell us that his boat was an old lady – almost fifty years old. 'Only two were ever built. Her sister boat was sailed across the Atlantic to New York by the designer who built her in Poole in 1971.'

That afternoon we crossed the island to a wonderful isolated white sandy beach, there was no one else to be seen. We discovered pieces of fishing nets and buoys which had been washed in by the tide, but sadly no treasures. Hector had a collection of shells, pieces of driftwood and interesting pebbles worn smooth by the sea in his cottage.

After supper that evening, we encouraged Hector to tell us more about Memec. He didn't take much persuading. 'Memec is a very safe boat and fast. I have achieved speeds of just over eighteen knots in good strong winds and a flat sea. She has a relatively short mast which is why she is so safe even in strong gale force winds. Her centre of gravity is quite low and close to the sea which prevents her from capsizing. I have owned her for about thirty years – before that she had done a lot of successful offshore racing especially the British, Three Peaks Race, which she won on three occasions amongst others. When I bought Memec I had a lot of fun sailing her with different crews over the years. One of the things I really like about sailing is you feel closer to nature depending on the wind and the tides of the sea. I also feel a strong sense of being a free spirit as you move along in full sail.'

We sat in front of a roaring fire which Hector fed at intervals with paper from a huge pile at the side of the fireplace. When asked what the papers were, he replied, 'Oh, they're just old accounts which need disposing of.'

Hector had recently returned from a trip to Galway in Ireland to visit his dentist. He was soon in full story mode telling us of his adventures. On this occasion he had taken a crew mate with him. His companion was the husband of a long-term friend who had been suffering from depression. Hector agreed that Edmund should go along for the ride. As they rowed out to Hector's trimaran, they both observed the swirling mist above the skyline which was magnificent. Although Hector had completed this journey many times, the sky and sea looked different every time. Always full of surprises, abundant wildlife occupied the sea. Seals and their pups galore on the outcrop of rocks, porpoises and whales soon surrounded the yacht. It must have been therapeutic for Edmund.

Hector reflected, 'As we journeyed on, I thought of my friend, Philippa who lives down the coast from me. She plays her fiddle to the seals. She has published a book telling of her experiences.' Hector presented us with a copy of the book some time later as a gift, which we still enjoy perusing from time to time. We discovered that Philippa was a conservationist and sometimes took abandoned seal pups home and had even kept them in her bath.

The first part of Edmund and Hector's journey was uneventful and took them north before they turned westward hugging the coast of Northern Ireland. Everything was 'plain sailing!' The sea was as calm as a mill pond. As they neared County Donegal, Hector noticed a slight change in wind direction and the sea became increasingly choppy. Edmund, who was not an experienced sailor became anxious. In no time the wind rose to near gale force. The local radio warned of winds up to forty-five knots approaching. As my late grandfather once described even when on a much larger ship, 'The boat was buffeted like a matchstick on the waves.' Hector described how the wind built and began to howl and pummel the boat like a hidden fist. Time to act and make an unplanned stop at Tory Island just eight nautical miles off the Donegal coast. Hector managed to contact the harbour master and got clearance to enter the shelter of the harbour wall. He was told there was plenty of room to moor his yacht safely as the ferry from the mainland had been cancelled.

They made their way up the sloping causeway. The wind blew against them, making them double over, but they were both very relieved to have solid ground beneath their feet. Strains of lively music competing with the cries of the wind reached them. Finally, after an epic struggle, they succeeded in forcing open the heavy oak door, of what turned out to be the local hostelry. Twelve pairs of eyes were transfixed on them. A man with a ruddy weathered complexion beckoned them over, 'Welcome to Tory Island you'll be in need of a wee dram.' Hector and Edgar readily accepted the offer. Once they had been served their drinks, an accordion struck up a few chords, sea shanties with a rousing chorus which most of the assembled crowd joined in.

It later transpired that the man who had offered them the first drink, no doubt one of several that evening, was the last king of the island, Patsy Dan Rodgers. Patsy had taken up the role in September 1992, on the death of the previous incumbent. He had been nominated by the son and daughter of the former king. The whole community of approximately one hundred and thirty people had voted him in unanimously. He accepted the honour and told his wife that he intended to go down to the pier every day to welcome people arriving on the island.

Hector and Edmund spent a comfortable night at a cottage recommended by one of the locals.

The following morning the sun was shining brightly, and all trace of the previous days' storm had disappeared. A few fishermen were mending their nets on the quayside. The single street of the village had a collection of houses which were either old and decrepit or newly renovated. They asked a local builder who was working on some scaffolding, about the tall stone derelict tower which dominated the view to the north of the village. 'That's the old bell tower and all that remains of a monastery founded by St Columba.'

As they were about to take their leave of Tory Island, they noticed an art studio, where several local artists exhibited their work. Hector always liked visiting art and craft venues and could not resist paying a visit. The young artist whom they spoke to told them how Derek Hill, an English artist had mentored several of the island's now internationally recognised painters. These artists had had exhibitions not only in Dublin and Edinburgh but in New York. The artist community included Patsy Dan Rodgers their host from the previous evening. It was a pity that none of his work was currently on sale.

Hector phoned his dentist in Galway to explain his delay and managed to rearrange his appointment. Hector and Edmund examined the trimaran and found no damage. They left the harbour and set course for Galway Bay. As they sailed down the Donegal coastline, they passed the distant shores of Sligo and Mayo. Just a dimple on the skyline was Ben Bulben. We later learnt, on a family holiday to Sligo, that Yeats, had once been a sailor, and was buried at the foot of the mountain. On his tombstone is the epitaph, 'Cast a cold eye on life, On death horseman pass by.' As it was now well past our usual bedtime, we retired to bed satiated by all of Hector's stories and knowing that we had an early start to catch the ferry the following morning.

I recently searched the internet for background details about Tory Island and found that Patsy Rodgers had died in 2018. There is an interview on You Tube with an American radio station where he spoke of the hardship of the inhabitants of the island and many were leaving for the mainland. Patsy appears to have been a larger than life character and it is no wonder that Hector thought well of him.

In a recent 'WhatsApp' message from Hector he told us that his trimaran had suffered badly last Autumn and had been damaged, whilst at anchor in the harbour but fortunately not beyond repair. He is currently looking into having it repaired. Hector is now fully computer literate unlike twenty years ago when he shunned modern technology. He has the latest i-phone and sends us thousands of photos via 'WhatsApp' of his latest exploits. His son, Hamish has initiated him in the wonders of modern gadgetry, and he is now very much part of the twenty-first century.

Make a List of Those You Will Hug

Matthew Harper-Hardcastle

Make a list of those you will hug
of those you will run to when not stopped by this
bug
sat tight, all close, interlinked, snug
nattering, hot tea, hands clasped 'round a mug.

Make a list of all the smiles that you miss
All the hellos you wish you could give with a kiss
All the giggles you can still hear from across the
abyss
Because one day we will talk of more than just this.

Make a list of the all food you will munch
All the friends you wish you could have over for
lunch
The smell of fresh coffee that still packs a punch
One day you'll have your besties over for brunch

Make a list of all the things you will keep.
That walk, that quiz, that routine for sleep
How you saved money from doing things on the
cheap
How you became a good neighbour by making that
leap

So when you struggle to muster more than a shrug
And no lift can come from any song, any drug
Take a breath, look up, lie down on the rug
And make a list of those you will hug.

Closed Door

Anon

Every time you put me down, It hurts me to my core,
Every time you ignore me,
It cuts even deeper.
My confidence lost,
My mood is so low,
I think about my future... And I don't want to know.
I look right behind me,
At all the hurt and the pain,
And it stresses my heart out with so much anxiety,
When I hurt once again.
I never spoke to you like that.
I listened when you called.
I don't know if I can face tomorrow, I feel so
unloved.
I can't trust my extended family To care for my soul,
They threw it away
To achieve their own goals.
They damaged my property,
And stole many things,
But what hurts the most are the Assumptions that
mental illness brings.
"You'll never be worthy,
You are in the **underclass,**
You won't hold a job down
And your marriage will never last. You shouldn't
have children,
You could never make a home,

I'll give you a label
And attack you with ECT when you're feeling at
your most vulnerable And very let down.
I'll take away your liberty,
I'll make you stay inside,
I'll take away your job from you,
Or punish you so much at work that you'll lose all
your pride.
Someone might know you,
But they don't like your name.
Believing all the stories that have given you **So...
much .... pain.**
You can't run away,
There's **always** an elephant in the room.
You can never let go of the pain that constantly
Physically hurts you.
You'll sweat through the nights, Thinking, "Do I
deserve such pain?" You feel so unworthy,
You want to throw your life away.
Down you are sliding,
You can't seem to stop,
As your low mood gains momentum, You're waiting
for the crash.
I look back at my school days,
I was happier back then,
But still carrying a load on my back
From the sharpest hurt and pain, that hurt me so
deeply, although it's now been and gone.
I've fallen so fast,
I'm in the Underclass now,
My feelings don't matter.
I feel so much worse,

I don't really feel loved

Even the people who helped me before, Have moved on and gone away,

Finally all that I can see in my future is **A firmly closed door.**

Lockdown

Joanne Platt

Go straight home they told us. So I ran. Burst open the door.

My mother was in the kitchen. A fat tear sat on her cheek so I guessed she'd been cutting onions.

I saw the sailboats bobbing in the window pinned against the sky. Wings white, flat to the sun like bedsheets. The square in shadow. A wedge shaped patch of light signalling towards the old town. The silhouette of a girl with pigtails cut suddenly across it chasing her hoop. I leaned over to see her face but she wasn't anyone I recognised from my school.

I put my satchel away in the cupboard where my mother put the Christmas decorations.

My mother always smelt of flowers. Even her apron was covered with flowers.

The men with their barrows have stopped coming. Before the barrows it was the vans. Black. Eyeless. Indiscernible against the falling shadows.

The plants are dead. All of them. There I've said it! Dead. Dead. DEAD.

Curled up like brown paper. Mouldered. Rotten.

One day the sun came and danced in the town square. A patch of sunlight blazing on the living room wall like a lit match. A little old man stepped out. He came most days after that. Stood under the carved arch that survived through all the demolitions, through the building of the new residential blocks like a beached galleon guarding the entrance to the old town.

At times I doubted he was real. A ghost? A future gone? God knows there were enough restless souls rattling around there by then.

Those were the times I'd hear my mother's voice chide me

Smell her flowers

The next day I took out my paints and I painted my mother.

I didn't paint at all the day after that.
Nor the next.

Nothing could paint away that stench.

It must have been the seventh day that the man made contact. Beckoned to me from the harbour. I was ready to go.

I still don't know what changed my mind like that right there at the last moment. But if something hadn't I wouldn't have been there to see it. Our balcony suddenly aflame with golden coral sunlight. Rays emanating from a centre of livid pink.

The silvery green spikes of my cactus.

Over the unswept carpet I crawled then until I was close enough to reach out and curl my fingers round the kitchen door.

I knew already what I was going to find. Still it came as a shock. My mother lying on the kitchen floor. Her hands clasped together as if in prayer. And no longer that unbearable mouldered blue, but gilded over with the most intense, the most saturated colours from my paintbox. And the cactus flower sat where her mouth was like a butterfly.

Six Months of Daily Walks
Helen Kenwright

January

The white protects
　　　　　　with spikes:
The frozen armour
of the sleeping world.

February

I walk home from a meeting
Four people
Four agendas
Two hours
One list
Two voices
No decisions

Four people
Going nowhere
And I'm holding the map
No-one wanted to see.

March

Mountains heaped like
A duvet
On the bedrock
Soft folds protecting
The earth's tender places
While she sleeps

April

Alone with the trees
My bones are unstuck
My body moves freely
Like a bike with the brakes off
I'm freewheeling.

May

Pink and white streaks across
A pale blue sky
Silhouette of flying bird
Gliding.

June

Sun hits my skin
Dandelions drifting
The start of summer.

Life goes on.

Mildred
Sue Richardson

Mildred Fortescue climbed aboard the bus the local supermarket had provided for the elderly whilst the virus was in the country. Normally Mildred would pop to the shop under her own steam, but since her age group had to be protected, the weekly bus was her only journey out of her small bungalow in Filey. The virus had changed her whole routine. Mildred normally went to the bridge group on Monday. Tuesday was her day to tend her small garden and so far she had been allowed to do this. Now though she felt that would soon be banned. The world had gone mad – totally utterly mad! Mildred mumbled 'hello' to the driver. The keeping-a-distance business was so annoying for her. Taking a seat at the rear, she nodded to Mrs. Davis who lived just around the corner.

The bus started to move. Two people, Mildred thought. Two flipping people. How on earth was this to end? Would she never go swimming at the beach again? Would they keep them behind closed doors until the elderly all died and did the government a favour? No one was going to keep her behind doors. She decided tomorrow she was going down to the beach for a swim. She had swum in the sea since she was a small child – she and her father had gone every Saturday until her teens when she took up dancing . In fact, she had been remarkably fit until her heart showed some problems last year – a touch of angina the doctor had told her. So Mildred had taken care she still swam but used the local pool on Thursdays as the session was free to the over seventies. But last week they also closed that.

"Keeping nice weather today, isn't it, Laura?" Mildred shouted from the rear of the bus.

"Yes. Are you hoping to buy toilet roll? My Derek said I'd to buy twenty packs just to annoy the security." Laura let out a loud chuckle.

"No, I'm fine for that. I just need some potatoes and milk really as I have plenty. It's mostly to get out as I'm fed up. It's all *their* fault!"

"Whose fault, Mildred?"

"Those flipping Chinese. All of them. I'm not allowed to go to my bridge class. I'm not allowed to go to the beach since those teenagers had that barbeque. Well I am going to the beach tomorrow and let the flipping police arrest me. The chief constable is a member of my bridge club!"

"Here we are," shouted Bill the bus driver.

Mildred picked up her shopping bags and climbed off the bus.

"See you both soon," shouted Bill.

Mildred pushed the small trolley into the supermarket where lots of staff were wearing gloves and masks. She went over to the fruit and veg section. She picked up some apples.

"Must get bananas," she mumbled under her breath. Glancing over towards the section with bananas, she saw *him*!

The cheek of it, she thought. You would think when this virus was in Britain, *he* would either stay in or go back to his country.

"Look at him, look at him," she said aloud. "That's it – he takes all the food too. Beansprouts – yeah that's all you eat – flipping bean sprouts."

Mildred's temper was rising.

"I'll beansprout you," she said.

Mildred picked up a large cabbage and took aim – it flew over the heads of the other shoppers. Then, thud. It hit the head of the young male employee who was stacking tins of baked beans. Down he fell, causing many gasps from people. Time seemed to stand still. Mildred stood, mouth open. An announcement came through the tannoy, loudly over her head.

"First aider needed in the veg section. First aider please."

"Mr. Wong, can you assist me?" the manager said.

"Do you know him?" Mildred asked the manager.

"Yes, he is a surgeon at York Hospital. Was it you who caused this? You could have killed him!"

"I'm sorry. It's just I've been locked up, so to speak. I'm not allowed to play bridge or swim."

"You're not allowed to play bridge!? Good God, woman. People are dying and all you can do is attack one of my staff."

"I wasn't trying to hit the young man. I was trying to hit him." Her voice wobbled as she spoke. "He was taking all the bean sprouts."

"I was taking the beansprouts because I'm making quick stir fry meals for the A&E staff." Mr. Wong spoke with a deep Yorkshire accent. "Our patient will live, no thanks to you. He will need to go to hospital, and be checked over in case he has concussion."

"I am really sorry," she said. "Am I going to be arrested?"

"I'm not sure," said the manager. "It's a serious thing you have done. You can't go around attacking people because they are Chinese. For one, it's racist, and look at what you could have done." He pointed towards the young man who was now awake, though seemed dazed. "I think you need to apologise, not only to Wilf, but to Mr. Wong. It's quite lucky for Wilf that Mr. Wong was here. A fine surgeon he is too."

Mildred felt her face redden with embarrassment. How would she ever face anyone again? The paramedics were now walking towards the small crowd that had gathered.

"I think you all need to move away and adhere to the social distancing rules please," said the manager.

They popped Wilf onto a trolley and spoke briefly to Mr. Wong. Both gave Mildred a stare of disgust before leaving the store.

"I am really sorry," Mildred said. "I will never be so ridiculous again. And if I can pay for the food you have bought for the doctors and nurses at the hospital, I'd like to do so if I may."

Broken

Angi

I remember as a child sitting
watching my grandmother unravelling
wool from worn-out, outgrown jumpers
then knitting something new.
Cutting cloth into geometric shapes
or thin strips, turning the old and discarded
into material for quilts or rugs.

Back then she would listen to friends and family
putting the world to rights
over cups of tea and slabs of homemade cake.

Now we live in a throwaway world
of built-in obsolescence,
where robots have replaced humans to create
soulless, 'must-have' goods
(at least for the next six months)
until a 'better' model comes along.

A world in which people text not talk
and live their lives in a virtual bubble
never really connecting in a meaningful way.

Without the craftsman's loving touch
the careful make do and improve,
without interaction over tea and cake –

these stalwarts of the past,
is there any wonder why the poor and dispossessed,
the sick and broken people are likewise thrown away
on the rubbish dump of life?

Arclight Trials

Ross Clements

[This is an extract from the beginning of a story.]

The woman who called herself the Queen handed him a cup of tea. This was not what he expected when he got the catalyst for the "Queen of the Storm". Dark, curly hair that went down to just below her shoulders, her eyes a light pink and a dainty feminine nose on her face with tanned skin bordering on chestnut, she was not what he was expecting. He wasn't even expecting her to be human, she was supposed to be a dragon for crying out loud!

"So," Richard began, "is this your true form?"

"What of it?" the Queen replied.

"It's just… I really don't see them accepting my application to join the Red Ghost Unit unless I summon a creature with real combat capabilities. Can't you transform into something fearsome?"

The Red Ghost Unit were the true elite. The war against Blackvale would have been lost ages ago if it weren't for the Red Ghost Unit. Arclight's finest, they all were masters of combat magic that could go into situations with odds deemed impossible to an ordinary military platoon and come out on top.

Richard Dartz struggled to live up to his family name. While previous members of the Dartz lineage included the likes of Cornelius Dartz, the peerless warrior who mixed battle magic with pure martial prowess, making a name for himself in the history books for his role in the Arclight Revolution, and Tabitha Dartz, who could lock down the battlefield with a myriad of creatively wielded curses, Richard never really measured up to his ancestors. Despite all the support that he received from his parents, Richard was a rather lacklustre Weaver of the arcane. His potions were inert, his pyromancy failed to send a flame further than one metre. It was clear that when compared to his peers, the only reason he had been allowed to progress so far was because of nepotism. The Red Ghost Unit did not have anyone who bought their way in. Every single member had their worth on the battlefield.

The Queen wrinkled her nose. "If I am to be summoned, I should think it would be for a matter of great importance. It is bad enough to be summoned by such a novice in the first place. Why do you need to join this Red Ghost Unit enough to enlist the support of a queen?"

Richard set down his tea. "Well, I didn't know that I would be summoning the Queen herself, I was just hoping to summon one of your lesser dragons or maybe a draconic knight at most. To answer your question though, it is an honour to be a part of the Red Ghost Unit. They are instrumental in this war. This is my chance to finally make something of myself."

"So, it is merely for personal glory then? I hardly think the ambitions of some fledgling Weaver are something that I need to concern myself with."

"Don't you understand? This isn't just personal glory; the Red Ghost Unit are necessary for this war. People are dying and food supplies are running low."

"If people are in such dire need of sustenance, why not become a farmer?" she asked. "If people need additional manpower why not raise a family?"

"I…I can't become a farmer! A Dartz becoming a farmer is just ridiculous!"

"So, it is personal glory then. You are happy to serve your country if it will gain you renown, but tilling the fields and sowing seeds is beneath your family name. I will not 'transform' for you. I may respect you as my summoner, but I am not a dog or a circus animal to perform tricks on your behalf. You may present me before this Red Ghost Unit if you wish, but I will reserve my power for when I am presented a worthy task, and that is my final answer."

It was clear to Richard that there was no further debate to be had here, this was all the cooperation he was going to get. "Fine," he conceded, "I will re-summon you before the committee. Until then."

The difficult part of summoning is the initial summon. Subsequent summonings of the same being or individual are a simple matter of activating the recording of the talisman involved in the original summon. This talisman is also able to be used to dismiss the creature until you need them again.

Richard Dartz invoked the power of his talisman and dismissed the Queen. He would need to summon her in front of the lieutenant for his application. He went over to his liquor cabinet and got himself a single scotch. He surely deserved it after this ordeal. So that was Queen Tempryca. Well, I've done what I can, I just need to hope for the best when we convene. Just three days.

So began the partnership between Richard Dartz and Tempryca, Queen of Storms.

Stinkhorn Search

Adam Parfitt

[An extract from a memoir in progress.]

I am unsure as to whether it was the lack of sleep due to watching Vikings until 0333 or a moment of sudden inspiration, but now things make sense. Is this why I failed to attend to my morning ablutions?

My landlord, Nicholas, always discouraged me from running in the woods. He said, with a stutter, that it was because he has pest control people in there and he did not want me getting shot accidentally. Maybe there was genuine concern or maybe he was protecting something.

This morning I kind of trespassed. Is it trespassing to walk through an open gate and to literally follow your senses? If so, I am a bad man, but I would do it again, every day. The draw of the stinkhorn was too strong. I love it. It strikes my nasal chords so much I feel giddy. It has a distinct rotten smell designed by nature to attract flies. They distribute its tiny spores by landing on the cap which get attached to their feet. Most people find it a revolting and repulsive smell, but I find it intoxicating. The arrival of the stinkhorn is something I look forward to annually.

Walking through the woods felt amazing; my feet getting wet when they rubbed against the dewy blades and the noises, they were astounding. I found peace in simple sounds. Billie and Bobbie buzzard calling overhead, the distant mooing of the dairy cows in the nearby field, and the creak of the pines blowing in the wind. I became aware that there truly is beauty in the detail; nature's treasures – fungi – they were everywhere. Oh, the joy of the hunt. I picked up the odd stinkhorn scent, but then as I tried to home in, it would float away as quickly as it appeared. Ferns covered the ground making it hard to use sight to pinpoint it. I was amongst the avenue of oaks, flanked by pines, all in lines. Just one of the secrets my landlord did not want me to find.

All this joy was suddenly interrupted by a storm in my guts and I knew not what to do. Do I run back to the cottage or do I engage with nature in the most primal of ways? It was a simple decision, the urgency was pressing, my pants were down and within seconds I had left my mark. The relief was instantaneous, and leaves helped in place of the toilet paper I take for granted. Now I could be bitter and feel shameful, but if my recent diagnosis of Irritable Bowel Syndrome (IBS) has shown me one thing, it is that sometimes I have no control over things.

However, if I did not have IBS, I would not have experienced the joy of Pooing in the Woods!! :-D I recommend it. The vulnerability, and the fear felt, explains why dogs have a strange look on their face when they are laying a load. For me, the prospect that I might get shot by the pest control guy added another layer of excitement.

I continued my sensory exploration and found the true secret Nicholas was keeping from me. A ten-foot-high fence surrounding some trees. An umpire's chair, for Mr Pest Control, and an electrified fence. A gate secured with plastic straps, no locks. Is it a game or is it not? I know not but maybe.

I returned home, unsuccessful in my hunt for stinkhorns, but safe in the knowledge that I had found a reason for the defensiveness and lies. I did not want to anger the gods, aka my landlord, and left it to explore another day.

.

My Berceuse
Llykaell Dert-Ethrae

And when Death opened up his hand

I saw it clear as day that he

held a pen made from my own blood.

And as he put the pen to the page

I felt my veins open up

and saw my own soul within his book.

Now that my name is written down inside

that venerated tome of his

I know that I am his forevermore.

My life is bound

my blood is his

and I stand naked at the gate

within in his arms

our hands entwined

far past the veil

into the swell.

I gladly go with a pure smile

and a tear down my ravaged cheek.

Here at the end

he has my all

far beyond the sky

up through the squall.

I cannot see where this will lead

but I know peace within the bonds

that hold me close

to all his bones.

And the cold caress that I embrace

whispers my name

I answer him:

his every bid a joy to me.

He lays me down and I obey

inside the dark

of our midnight.

There I am taken by the night

shining from the sky down to the earth.

And I rest now within his arms

ink on the page

my berceuse.

Mirror Mirror on the Wall
Lynne Parkin

On the outside, Twenty-Six Baker Crescent looks like the rest of the sweeping four-storey houses. From the street, the house oozes opulence, but on the inside it is a different story. When you walk through the front door into the hallway and touch the walls at any point you can feel it breathing, laboured breathing that would send a shiver down anyone's spine. The ground and first floors are filled with exquisite furniture from around the world, including a sofa from Tibet, rugs from India in the living room and silk curtains and throws from Japan in the bedrooms, with artefacts from far flung places placed on shelves, dressers, windowsills and walls.

Professor Stanley Faulks, Archaeologist, and owner of the house spends months at a time away from home. He shares number Twenty-Six with his wife Judy a barrister, who is either at work, in court or knee deep in cases in her office at home. If you do not know them, you will be forgiven for thinking that they are the only occupants.

In the attic rooms live the couple's fourteen year old twins Elsie and Edward. Are they typical fourteen-year olds? No. Are they typical twins? That depends on how you define typical. Elsie dislikes her life. She hates school, life at home and having to spend time alone with her brother. Edward hates Elsie because she was born first. Petty, but it is simmering unnaturally in his brain and he hates his parents for having twins. Are they children with issues? Possibly. Well liked? Definitely not. Private school educations do not always foster friendships. In fact they can often breed something unhealthy. On the whole Stanley and Judy keep themselves to themselves. The few friends that they claim to have, are like themselves, academics. They do not enjoy outside pleasures and they keep their children at a distance indoors, except for breakfast.

In amongst the beauty of the rooms there is an air of… well foreboding. It creeps around the furniture and rooms, seeping down into the walls and floors, amassing in the basement. It is only sensed on rare occasions by a few like-minded academics who are occasionally honoured with an invite. They don't know what it is and are too afraid to ask. Professor Stanley and Judy Faulks cannot explain anything they sense, which is not surprising, as they are always locked in their own little worlds of work; thinking about archaeological digs and high profile court cases. Do the children notice? Subliminally maybe.

Monday to Friday between 6.30am and 7.30 am is breakfast time in the Faulks household, the only shared event in their lives. It is a necessity for Judy so she can say, 'we talk over breakfast.' Ask the twins, they will say NOTHING. If it makes her feel better then so be it. Will it make Elsie and Edward feel better? No! It's just a time and place to eat. Then bags collected, they jump into the Jaguar and she drops them at school. Acutely aware of the interaction of the other parents and their children, she smiles at the twins unnaturally and waves animatedly as they walk away.

'Bitch!' Edward growls under his breath. 'You are so alike.'

Elsie turns in a flash and glares at him. 'What are you going on about baby brother?'

'Nothing to concern you Elsie,' he hisses. 'Wind your neck in and mind your own business.'

Turning away from him Elsie scowls. Then a smile breaks out on her face. She knows how much he hates her calling him baby brother. Life at this precise moment is peachy.

The day for Edward goes slowly. The clock on the wall seems slow yet his thoughts respond to the noise it makes, working in time to the tick tock, tick tock. His fellow pupils were just that, pupils. There is no connection between he and them at all. School is not a place for Edward, not in the beginning, not now, not ever.

Elsie, on the other hand is eagerly drawing in her exercise book. The drawings are exceptionally detailed, but have nothing to do with the maths lesson that she is currently in. She looks around the classroom which is full of idiots, inferior beings with large pocket money purses, horses, chauffeurs and holiday homes across the globe. She glowers as her eyes stop at the tall excuse for a human being which is her teacher Mr Michaels. What an ignorant prat, an amoeba in life's murky pond. She does not like him at all and from their first meeting decided that he did not warrant her attention. Nothing changes.

Following the indignity of having to catch a bus home after school because Mother is in court, the twins raid the kitchen cupboards for crisps and biscuits and take their finds to their rooms on the fourth floor, without saying a word to each other. They slam then lock their bedroom doors in unison. They have more in common than they realise.

Elsie's room is rather dark with a mural of herself in a dark dress and cloak standing on a rock in the middle of a roaring sea looking down at an illuminated apple in her hand. There are wolves and mystical beasts on the other walls. On her dressing table she has an assortment of goblets and relics from a bygone age, borrowed from her father's store of artefacts. Elsie calls him Stanley, he is not worthy of the title of father. Is she worried that he may venture up the servants stairs to her room? No he never has and she is sure he never would. Above the dressing table is a large wooden mirror, which is covered in gold leaf. Elsie takes out her work book from her bag and stares intently at the drawings. Actually they are more like diagrams. She smiles as her fingers follow the lines her pencil has made earlier in the day. Taking a block of black ink and a brush she transferred the diagrams onto her ideas wall. She feels satisfied. Life can only get better, she tells herself. No one will get in her way!

Edward on the other hand is already tucking into his stash. He doesn't know when his mother will be back home and if he didn't have a hunger to feed he wouldn't care. His room too is dark. There is a mirror in the corner propped, face inwards, against the wall. Edward does not like the mirror but is too afraid to get rid of it. Will he admit that he's afraid? No! The walls are covered in diagrams which he doesn't understand. He does believe however that his life can be whatever he makes it. No one will get in his way! He sits on the floor and takes a box from under his bed. The box is full of bones, a goats horn, a lambs skull, a birds beak, a ravens wing, the list goes on. He places them in the order he always places them and smiles. Fragile as they are he has a place for each one but he is unsure why he puts them where he does. They are from the days when he could roam the woods and collect such things. Nowadays if he isn't at school, he is at home.

In the basement where all is darkness and evil prevails, candles burn brightly reflecting in a large ornate mirror, which leans proudly against the wall. Another day of unrest and unease for the… what? It looks like a spartan room belonging to a down and out, but it can't be. Not in the house of opulence. Down there is a chill that cuts to the bone. Alongside the turbulent unease, is the heavy breathing. There is no getting away from it, unlike the walls in the rest of the house, once it reaches the basement you feel it tenfold. If you venture in there that is. Looking around the room there are no indicators as to who the occupant is. Questions linger in the air. Who are you? Why do you light the candles? Where are you now? It is not to ask these questions for interest purposes but to distance yourself from the evil the room exudes.

Evening arrives, no mother, but there is the familiar knock of the man from the fish and chip shop down the road bringing their supper. He does it as a favour because their mother has helped him with legal issues in the past. Elsie opens the door and thanks him. Then tossing her brothers wrapped supper at him they eat hurriedly leaving the empty wrappers on the table and race upstairs without speaking.. Then you hear the usual slamming of doors and keys turning in locks. Time for bed?

Edward sits on his chair and looks at the floor, he feels sure that the objects have been moved slightly. He is a little unnerved by this and hurriedly moves them back into place so that his bed is surrounded. From the corner of his eye, he sees one of the diagrams on the wall by the door turn itself around. That is enough to send Edward rushing for his bed, as he does so he trips and catches his forehead on the bedpost, which sends a gush of blood onto the eagles skull directly below it.

'Shit!' he shouts.

He doesn't care. In bed he pulls the covers over his head, then he feels for his torch which is under his pillow. Something un-nerving is in the air and he doesn't mind admitting to himself that he doesn't like it.

In her room Elsie smiles, she is sitting at her dressing table when she hears Edwards kerfuffle and expletive. What a wimp! That is why she was born first, she is superior, always will be. Sitting at her dressing table she turns her thoughts to the business of the evening. She has been waiting for this moment for a long time. What she needs is a binding spell and for this she thanks her school library and the book of spells found on the miscellany shelf. She opens the book at the correct page. Elsie takes her 3" by 3" piece of thick paper, taken from her mother's blotter in her office and a pen which is ideal for spells. She finds and writes the name of her victim on it. Then crossing the name with an inverted pentacle, she folds the paper in two, takes a deep breath and places the paper on her temple. Elsie repeats the following spell three times. Concentration is a must…

'To be protected from you, this magic charm I will do, with these words I bind thee, for you to let me be, to be protected from your harm, I now seal this charm.'

Putting the piece of paper on the floor Elsie visualizes the person. She stamps her foot on the paper, nine times in total and after each one she says, 'So shall it be.' Once this is done, Elsie sighs. There are two things about this spell that she doesn't know and they are: where that person needs to be for it to work on them and how long it lasts. She does however know that it is placed on the intended person and has been a long time coming.

The silence that is shrouding Edward halts his breath momentarily and he shivers. He feels restrained and helpless. There are strange things in the night that he does not have a hold of. After dark, night-time noise breaks through the silence. Noises that he is not a part of. They are oppressive and leave him with a fearful spirit. Tonight the amplified voice of his sister rattles around the fourth floor but her words are muffled. He pictures in his mind's eye the bones surrounding his bed, not one out of place. Is he safe for now? He doesn't know. Sleep does not come easy, it never comes easy. When it does, it is fretful.

Laying on her bed Elsie smiles, satisfied with her

work. 'This is just the beginning, the very beginning.' She purrs with satisfaction. Sleep for Elsie comes easy oh so easy. 'Goodnight world.'

BANG! The sound reverberates around the house, not from the street outside but inside - yet it is unrecognisable. It isn't a slammed door or window, nor their mother clattering about due to her anger or frustration. The noise woke Elsie immediately and she is annoyed. Whoever or whatever is responsible for this intrusion will suffer. Edward on the other hand was still awake and is now more frightened than earlier. What is going on? Sitting on the edge of her bed Elsie gathers her thoughts. The mirror on her wall is illuminated. Cutting through the dark, the light draws Elsie towards it until her hand is touching the fragile glass. The mirror is filled with candles. Pulsating through her hand to her heart she is sharing thoughts with the unknown and she likes it. Now she knows what she must do.

Opening her bedroom door she shouts, 'Edward, Edward I need you.'

'No you don't,' he replies quickly. 'You've never needed me.'

'But it's different tonight, come on please.' She says.

He didn't want to tell Elsie that he was scared, it would mean her having a hold over him.

'I will look after you, I promise. I really will.' Elise is almost pleading. 'Come on, together we can make life more bearable.'

Edward scoops some of the bones from the floor and puts them in his pockets. He slowly opens his door to a point where he can see his sister. 'Well…'

'Will you look at your mirror?' she asks.

'No!' he replies. Without giving her question a second's thought.

'Please just look,' she says.

He turns slowly, his mirror is not facing him, it is still against the wall. 'I can't.'

Pushing past him Elsie runs to the mirror and with all her strength picks it up, turns it round and hangs it from the hook on the wall. Edward turns and is unsure of what he is seeing, and why. The mirror, his mirror, now illuminated, is flashing words one after the other – idiot, imbecile, second born, simpleton, underdog, overshadowed, the list went on. With every word something within Edward's soul dies and his head feels like it will burst. Yet he still doesn't understand. From nowhere he begins to sob and he doesn't care. Looking for understanding and comfort he seeks Elsie's gaze.

Composing herself she grabs Edward by the hand, moving swiftly towards the door, saying hurriedly, 'Into my room now. I will make all this stop for us, the bad words, the feelings.' Pulling him towards her he has no choice but to follow. He hasn't been in her room before and doesn't know what to expect. In fact, he is quite surprised to see that they have identical diagrams. Confused would best describe him at that moment.

'What's going on Elsie?' he asks. 'What have you done?'

'Something I should have done a long time ago,' she replies. 'But it's not over yet. We need to go down to the basement.'

'Oh no I don't think so.' Edward answers.. He feels the colour draining from his body and he has pins and needles in his hands and feet. His father tried often to take him down there and they hadn't been pleasant experiences. Each time he remembered running up the stairs and locking himself in his room. He wasn't followed, he never followed.

'I can't do this by myself Edward. Besides you don't want to be left in here with my mirror on your own, do you?

Edward glanced at her mirror which was still illuminated and shivered 'I could go into the kitchen and wait for Mother.'

Elsie speaks matter-of-factly. 'The last person you want to be waiting for is Mother believe me. She doesn't have our wellbeing at heart or anyone else's for that matter. Just her own'

Sighing Edward nods his head, 'Ok, you win.'

They run down the three flights of stairs passing the bedrooms, living rooms and kitchen with the final flight ending at the basement door.

'What now?' he whispers. 'Mother always keeps the door locked. I don't know why, you won't catch me down here. Well not normally.'

Reaching into her pocket Elsie pulls a large ornate key from her pocket. Showing it to Edward she then puts it into the lock. There is a grating sound as the key turns. Opening the door wide the first thing they see is a large ornate gilt mirror, surrounded by candles; the same candles they had seen in Elsie's mirror. Looking around the room she is pleasantly surprised. Edward on the other hand is shaking, he sees his mother sitting in a corner of the room, rocking backwards and forwards gently, her face is expressionless.

'What is going on and what is she doing down here?' he whispers to his sister.

'Oh don't you worry, she can't hurt you.' Elsie replies as she moves into the room. 'In fact I think you will find her quite subservient, isn't that right Mother?' There is no reply.

Edward has lots of questions in his head, but for now one would have to do. 'Why is she down here?'

'Why, to be with Father of course,' she replies. 'Well, that's what she thinks."

The whole situation is becoming very confusing for Edward. His father was away on some dig in the Far East. Seeing the look of puzzlement on his face, Elsie takes his hand once more and leads him back to the mirror.

'Tell me what you see in the mirror, little brother.'

Feeling a little braver, he peers into the mirror's depths and gasps, 'It's Father, is he coming back? I hope not, I hate him.'

'No, no,' Elsie says, 'Stanley is in the mirror. Entombed for all eternity.'

'But how?'

'Enough questions you are making me tired. I need to finish this right now.' She turns to her mother and continues talking as she walks towards her. 'Mother, and I use the term loosely, for you are anything but a mother. You play with our lives like we are toys. Well it is now time for us to play with you!'

Checking her mother's pockets she finds the basement door key wrapped in a handkerchief with her father's initials on it. She checks it then puts it back in the same pocket. Then she summons her brother to help move their captive to the mirror. As they hold her up Elsie whispers in her ear, 'No more will we be beholden to someone who doesn't care. You will live the rest of your life in silent purgatory, believing you are responsible for your husband's death. We will be free to be ourselves and not trophies to be talked about at law society dinners. Hate is a powerful thing and our hate is greater than any shown to you by those you have sent to prison for their crimes or those sent to the gallows for murder.'

Holding her mother tightly, Elsie takes the mirror and lays it flat on the floor between the candles. Then they stand their mother on it and smile. Bending their mother's head so she looks into the mirror they can see from her reflection her eyes moving from side to side in sheer panic. They take her back to her chair.

Elsie whispers in her ear, 'Remember this moment. Your last sighting of your beloved husband. But you know what you don't deserve each other because you messed up the lives of your two children.'

Feeling a little braver, Edward stands next to his sister. 'She's right, he is evil and you could have stopped him messing with my head – our heads.'

As they walked towards the door Elsie turns towards the mirror. Taking the key she hits the mirror with it, then watches it crack into a thousand pieces.

'Only we know the truth of the mirror,' she tells Edward, as she locks the door behind them. 'Others will just see a fractured piece of Victoriana.'

Running up the servants stairs, they both feel light hearted. It's as though they've had great weights lifted from them. They head straight into Elsie's room and sit on her bed.

'This is what will happen tomorrow,' she tells him. 'We will go to school as normal, on the bus. I will lose the key to the basement in the lake, during my rowing lesson. In passing I will mention to Miss Wilson that Mother did not come home last night. She will mention it to our head of year who will ring mothers chambers, and they will say she didn't turn up for work today. Police will come looking for clues, find the locked door in the basement and as there is only one key they will break the door down to find mother completely mad with a lot of candles and a broken mirror.'

Sometimes, for children, things in life can be as simple as they want to make them. With no regrets.

Real Life
William Davidson

Rita and Norman sat on the low wall near the War Memorial and took in the comings and goings on Duncombe Place. Their bus wasn't due for a few more minutes. Rita liked to watch people, but she knew Norman wasn't so bothered. He just wanted to get back home for *Pointless*. Taxis u-turned, Deliveroo riders sped past, tourists dawdled, trying to frame the perfect shot of the Minster at the end of the street.

'That's a big dog,' said Norman. 'A husky.'

Rita looked to see what Norman was talking about. It was a dog without a lead, trotting by the side of a large man in a long black coat. Rita couldn't abide people walking their dogs without leads. It was as if they were saying, 'I don't need a lead because this animal is entirely obedient to me.' It was distasteful.

'Best get on, Rita,' said Norman, drumming at his knees as if there were a song playing that only he could hear.

Rita kept watching the dog. But it wasn't a husky. She felt a tingling in her fingers.

'It's not a husky,' she said.

'Yes, it is, love,' said Norman, standing up and brushing invisible crumbs from his v-neck. 'Huskies are unmistakable.'

'Well, you're mistaken this time,' said Rita, getting up too, and turning for a moment to Norman. 'It's a wolf.'

'Ha!' said Norman. 'Very good. Now come on, we

haven't got long.'

'I'm serious,' said Rita. 'Look at it. Look at its narrow shoulders, its long tail.' It turned to hold their gaze for a moment. 'Its eyes, Norman. Its beautiful, wild eyes.'

'Rita,' said Norman, 'we are going to be late. If we miss this bus, we won't be home while six and it'll be over.'

'It's a wolf,' said Rita. 'Come on. Let's follow them.'

Rita set off after the man and the wolf. Norman made grumbling noises behind her.

'Stop, Rita,' he said. 'We'll miss the bus. We'll be too late.'

'Keep up, Norman,' said Rita. 'This is worth missing *Pointless* for. It's a wolf, Norman. A wolf. In York.'

'Nothing is worth missing *Pointless* for,' said Norman.

'*Pointless* will be on iPlayer,' said Rita. 'The wolf won't be. This is real life. A wolf in real life.'

'Oh God,' said Norman as they passed the Great West Doors of the Minster, 'it's not the same watching on the iPlayer. It's, you know, less exciting.'

The man and the wolf went through the open gate of Dean's Park. Rita and Norman followed.

'He won't get away with that,' said Norman. 'Dogs have to be on a lead in the park. The Minster Police will caution him.'

The man sat down on the octagonal stone bench that surrounded the sycamore tree. The wolf lay at his feet. Rita stopped and gripped Norman's arm.

'We're going to meet a wolf,' said Rita. 'Come on, Norman.'

'No, we are not,' said Norman. 'Because it's not a wolf.'

Norman turned around and headed back out of the park.

'And I refuse to miss *Pointless*. I simply refuse.'

Rita watched Norman retreat towards the bus stop. She turned again to the man and the wolf. She took small steps across the grass and sat down by the man.

'Is it…?' said Rita. 'Is it…?'

'She,' said the man. 'It's a she.'

'Is she…?' said Rita.

'Yes,' said the man, 'yes, she is.'

'Could I stroke her?' said Rita.

The wolf sat up and looked at Rita. Its eyes were golden.

'Well, as a rule, I'd say no,' said the man. 'But, for you, today, I'll say yes, give her a stroke.'

Rita brushed her palm along the back of the wolf. Its coat appeared sleek and short, but Rita found her hand sank between its soft hairs. The wolf closed its eyes for a moment and Rita did too, keeping her hand still against the warmth of its body. One of the peregrines screeched high above them from the Minster bell tower. A car horn sounded in a nearby street. A busker strummed a guitar somewhere close by. Rita opened her eyes again to see the wolf looking at her.

'Thank you,' said Rita to the wolf and then to the man, and she got up and walked back to the gate, a railing of which she gripped as she steadied her breathing and considered where she might go next.

Life, Love and Family
Christina

Sam was watching from the other side of the road. He knew he shouldn't be there, but he couldn't keep away. He didn't understand why Cassie had phoned him to say it was over a few weeks ago, with no real explanation. It had only been six months but it was the best six months he'd had in a long time. Selfish but true. It felt right; they'd seemed happy, or at least he thought they were. She'd even agreed to move in with him. Then POW! she'd blindsided him with that message and hadn't taken any of his calls since. He felt the tears; he felt embarrassed, he was hoping no one would see him.

Was he crying for his dad who had passed away just a few weeks ago? Although they hadn't been close recently (he knew he'd let him down the one time his dad had asked for help) there was nothing he could do now. Sam had put everything else ahead of family; his job was his life, and of course the money. His wife still though there was time for children, but he didn't want them so he'd had a vasectomy without telling her. He'd had occasional affairs which gave him the rush that seemed to be missing out of his life, but then he'd met Cassie and he realised what he'd really been missing.

She was gone now, and so was his dad's business. There was nothing he could do about that at the moment. He'd figure it out. The funeral was next week, he'd deal with everything after that.

As he started to turn, the office doors swung open and Cassie walked out. He'd almost shouted 'No!' aloud; she was smiling, holding someone's hand, and she looked so happy . She looked the way she looked with him only a few weeks ago. He couldn't see who the new guy was: he had his hood up. She glanced across the road, saw Sam. He smiled and gave a small wave; she looked sad, waved, turned away. He noticed the other guy had just kept walking. Odd. Sam thought he recognised him by his walk, but he couldn't be sure.

Cassie'd almost caught up with the guy as they turned the corner. Who was this person? Why him? Sam wondered yet again what he'd done.

'Right,' he thought, 'I'm going to get her back.' The thought that he knew this man kept niggling at him - it would come to him, it always did - but for now he was cold and hungry. I'll just …

He got his phone out and pushed a button. "Hello wife," he said. "I'm sad… no, I'm just cold and tired long day." He listened to her. "Lucky for you I'm on my way home right now, and I just wanted to tell you I missed you," he laughs. "Great, I'm really hungry, that sounds wonderful. "We'll snuggle down on the settee in front of the fire and watch one of the box sets." He smiles to himself and thinks about how clueless his wife is as he gets in the car to drive home.

Cassie

Cassie came out of the office feeling happy; happier than she'd been in quite some time. She had a new man in her life, and she'd just found out she won a promotion with a substantial wage rise. She would be Head of the Administration Department with six staff working alongside her at Donald and Sons Solicitors. She was also moving into her new flat tomorrow and today she'd changed all her personal phone numbers.

She was on her way to celebrate with her new friend, Tommy, when he whispered that Sam was standing across the road. He said he'd walk ahead and dropped her hand. She turned and saw Sam. He looked sad; she wasn't sure, but she thought his eyes looked red from crying. She was about to go over , but decided to wave and walk away. She had to think about Tommy: she felt that in time maybe something could come of this friendship. Tommy was the man who had stopped her making a dreadful mistake moving in with Sam. Sam didn't travel for business, Tommy had told her. Sam was married to a really wonderful woman who had no idea of what he was up to, about his little flat where he had his affairs. The flat that Cassie had been going to move into. Tommy had been honest and told her what Sam was really like. Apparently his wife idolised him and wouldn't listen when family tried to tell her. Cassie hurt – pain for the love that had grown between them; pain for the lies and deceit; pain for the woman she hadn't even known existed.

She hadn't known that Sam was Ted's son. Ted had always talked about his clever university boy who was his pride and joy, one day he'd introduce them - but then he stopped talking about him. Cassie hadn't wanted to ask in case it was something bad, but she had had the pleasure of meeting Wendy, his wife, who was a really kind hearted woman. Ted had told his wife about this lovely woman who he thought was making jobs up for him to help him in this tough time and how grateful he was. Wendy had felt miffed and told Ted she wanted to meet this paragon of virtue. When Wendy had met Cassie she loved her, a teenager living on her own after losing her family, going to college and working every hour she could so she had rent and food money, and she suspected could help them out.

Cassie was waiting for the executors to execute her parents Will, hoping she might have a little something to put away for a rainy day, but she felt they were really dragging it out as it had been over a year. Wendy took Cassie's full details and lo and behold, it was sorted out within weeks. Wendy just winked and said, "Ask no questions and I'll tell no lies."

She'd not seen much of Wendy recently but Ted always made a point of keeping in touch.

That's how she'd met Tommy,

She took Tommy's hand and turned the corner with a feeling of relief, wondering at the lightness she felt.

Sam slipped easily to the back of her mind as she thought about where they would eat. Tommy suddenly stopped and asked if she was OK.

"Yes," she said, "I was just wondering what we should eat."

She smiled, he smiled back. "Um how about steak and chips? Indian? Italian? Or you could come back to mine for bangers and mash, we could pick up some wine?" He looked at her. "But of course, if it's too soon…."

She thought about what he'd said. "Indian. Yes, Indian, and we can buy the beer at the supermarket next door while we wait for it.

"Back to mine then." He smiled and they walked off. He'd asked her to go to Ted's funeral next week but, she wasn't sure she was ready for that yet.

Ted had sent Tommy to do a few little jobs for Cassie. When Tommy had said Ted was sick she asked after him and let him in, and that's when things started to go horribly wrong. She'd been showing Tommy the little things that needed doing when, he stopped at some pictures she'd just put up of her and Sam, and Tommy said, 'That's my cousin. I don't understand. He's married.'

Cassie said, 'It can't be. He doesn't have a family, they disowned him when he wouldn't give them any money. My family died so he's like me, we only got each other, it can't, it can't be, I've been going out with Sam for over six months, we're moving in together at the end of the month he can't be married? Surely he would have said something to me? Are you sure?' Her eyes had filled with tears.

Tommy stayed as long as he could. Once she was ready to fall asleep on the settee, he told her he would return the next day. And he did.

Once Tommy had gone she got up and sent a text to Sam saying it was over, that she never wanted to see him again, not to contact her, he was a shit. That was it, it was over. After weeks of crying and eating herself into oblivion with the help of Tommy, she had finally almost got back to her old self.

Tommy

Tommy was a happy go lucky kind of guy, who ran his own building company. It had taken him years to turn the run-down business of his Uncle Ted into this multi million pound company.

But recently things in his life had changed. He'd never really been interested in long term relationships; he'd been too busy with the company and taking care of his Uncle Ted, who had only recently passed away, leaving everything to him. That had put his cousin's nose out of joint, but it's not like his cousin had helped out any; he'd never put any money or time into it or done any work over the last few years. Even when his dad nearly went under. The only thing he'd done was to hold his hand out for money to get him through university, holidays and to pay off any loans; and once he'd got his super doper job in the city, when he could have saved his dad who had asked for a loan for a few months, Sam said no. He'd said it wasn't a viable loan (what the hell ,he's his dad for god sake).

Tommy had all the paper work and records. His uncle had been a canny old guy, recording all the conversations he'd had with people so they couldn't take advantage of him. People mistook him for an uneducated man, but that was their mistake. He'd been educated through his life: he'd learned the hard way, and knew more than most about everything.

Tommy took out loans and spent every hour possible working. He'd started as an apprentice after school and weekends, working his way through every job on the site. His uncle had told him that if he wanted to run the business that's what he had to do. He also put time in doing his City and Guilds in plumbing, carpentry etc.. Ted was so proud of him: when he passed his exams he gave him fifty per cent of the business and left the rest to him on his death, which had come as a shock. Ted told him as he lay dying but, it would only become official once the Will was read after Teds funeral service. He would be responsible for his aunt's care until she passed away which would never be a problem as they'd been like parents to him since his family had died in an accident.

Things changed for Tommy just before his uncle died. He'd asked Tommy to visit a friend who was moving out of her flat, as she had a couple of things that needed doing. Ted explained that she'd been one of the few people who had stuck by him when he'd had trouble with the business; he also thought that she'd given him things to do to help him out. He'd never forgotten her kindness, so he'd made a point of helping her whenever she needed it. He gave Tommy her address and said that he must explain he was poorly but, she knew about Tommy and would recognise his face from the picture he'd shown her. Tommy smiled; he knew how proud his uncle was of him and he truly loved him for it. He said he'd go after work as the address was on his way home. And that was how he met Cassie who, by opening the door, had tipped his world upside down.

The Wife

'The wife' was how Sam referred to Lizzie, and she hated it. She'd met Sam at university; Lizzie had been top in their finance class and was also top in her legal classes. She hadn't decided what she wanted to do, lawyer or financial account or something else. When she met Sam he was so different, a gentleman, and he'd made her his number one priority.

He didn't talk about his family much. She'd come from a very loving family. She'd assumed he hadn't, but in fact that wasn't true. When she'd met Ted, Wendy and his cousin they couldn't have been kinder so she didn't understand why he spoke about them the way he did. She did feel there was a lot of jealousy, as he felt his dad had always had more time for his cousin, but, as she tried to explain to him, it was only because Sam was away at university, and Tommy was at school, and helping his dad in his spare time. As Lizzie said, you could see how proud he was of him, how Ted had helped him out all through university with his bills, spending money, paying his loans and more. Sam had said she didn't know anything. He told her to keep her opinions to herself in future. She and Sam seemed happy but he'd started to become distant, so to protect herself she decided to try and distance herself from him. So, for the next few months, she worked and worked on her degrees. She felt freer, and that was when she'd chosen to go into law. It was probably the first time he'd had an affair but, Lizzie didn't realise it at the time.

A couple of months later, Sam had turned up begging her to forgive him. She wasn't going to give him a second chance but, he said that he'd realised that he loved her and wanted to - yes you guess it - to spend the rest of his life with her. They got married a couple of months later, bought a really lovely flat, both passed their exams with distinction, both got super-duper jobs in the city as Ted would say proudly, and their life felt good.

Sam wanted children, she wanted her career; Lizzie relented and they tried. When she'd miscarried Sam had made her feel so bad, a failure. It was Wendy who took care of her - Sam said he had to go on a business trip for a couple of weeks. she knew something was off as he'd been behaving badly before she lost the baby, being jealous about the baby, saying she didn't love him as much anymore, which was ridiculous. Since then her love and respect for him was lost. Knowing what she'd learned from the family and other sources, she knew she wanted out. She'd pretended to be the same for appearances, but she had her own little plan and Lizzie was about to spring it.

The day of Ted's Funeral

Ted's Funeral had gone off reasonably well, considering all the little surprises.

Number one was for Sam, who looked completely knocked sideways when Tommy turned up with Cassie. When Lizzie asked him if he was okay, he said it had just hit him how much he was going to miss his dad ,and he'd been feeling off kilter for the last couple of days. He looked at her and said, "Thank god I've always got you Lizzie, yes, thank god," and he took her hand. She just gave him a little smile as they walked into the church.

Number two was for Sam. When he looked back for his mum, Wendy, she'd walked over and given Cassie a cuddle. How the hell did she know Cassie?

Number Three was for Sam as well: it was Tommy. He knew he had recognised that walk, just not who it belonged to, as he hadn't spent any time with him for ages. The man who stole his father (in his heart he knew it wasn't true) - but he really disliked him for getting his father back on track, when he'd let his father down.

More was to come after the service was over.

It went something like this.

Outside the Crematorium

People were milling around saying the usual things: how sorry they were, how wonderful Ted was, funny little stories about Ted, how beautiful the flowers were and so on. So Wendy invited everyone back to Ted and Wendy's House.

Ted and Wendy's House

Cassie and Lizzie were helping put the food out with Wendy and with a few of his aunties. Sam started to feel unwell, dizzy, nauseous, he felt like he was going to have a heart attack; his breathing was all over the place. He hid himself in his dad's shed to gain some composure.

Tommy was sorting out the drinks. This went on for a couple of hours. Lizzie had to go and find Sam as she was worried about him. People were asking after him, which played into her hands ,and after giving him a good telling off - at which he seemed relieved, which was a bit weird - back they trotted to the house.

Sam wanted to confess all to Lizzie but, not here not now – later, at home, he'd throw himself on her mercy and hope for the best. After all, she'd only have to know about Cassie, nothing else.

After a couple more hours, Tommy, Wendy and Sam were saying goodbye to the last of the guests while Lizzie and Cassie were clearing up the last of the dishes. Sam was on edge again and wanted to rush these people out of the house so he could go and see what was happening in the kitchen.

Tommy went into the kitchen. Cassie and Lizzie were talking about work; he caught the tail end of the conversation: Cassie had told her about her job and promotion and he heard Lizzie say she was going back to work but she hadn't told Sam yet. Tommy walked in and they stopped talking. Cassie asked if he was OK; He smiled and said he was now that everyone had gone, but he'd be even better once Mr Higgins the solicitor had read the Will. Wendy had wanted everyone in the Dining Room for the reading. Cassie said she didn't want to intrude, but that was what Wendy wanted so she went.

The Reading of the Will

Wendy sat at the head of the table, Mr Higgins sat at the end of the table, Sam and Lizzie one side and Tommy and Cassie the other. First Wendy spoke and said she knew what was in the Will and if anyone kicked off or complained, that person would lose everything that Ted had left them. There was a clause that negated anything left to them and she would implement it.

Ted had left some money to a couple of his favourite shelters for Dogs and Cats, and a homeless shelter that Wendy and he worked at in their spare time.

Ted was very canny as I said before; he made sure that everything he requested was signed for so that if anyone reneged they would have to return it to Wendy.

Wendy got his Wedding Ring, the house, everything financially they had tucked away and £10,000 pounds to have fun with.

Wendy had agreed that upon her death Sam, Tommy, and Lizzie would get a third share in the house (this was in Wendy's Will) and that the house could not be sold out from under Wendy before that time and no loans taken against it. Then it got down to the nitty gritty.

Ted had left 40% of his business to Tommy, (Tommy signed on the line accepting the forty percent.) He also got his gold bracelet and cuff links and ten thousand pounds.

Ted also asked Tommy to look after Wendy and

make sure she never went without (Tommy signed on the line agreeing to do what Ted had wanted.)

Sam got seventy five thousand pounds, his father's watch, chain and St Christopher, (he was waiting for more, but he wasn't going to get it). Sam was pissed, but didn't say anything as he thought he had the company ten per cent in the bag. By now everyone was signing on the dotted line.

Lizzie got twenty thousand pounds to do with what she wanted. Lizzie cried, she really loved that old man. He had spoken to her just before he got sick and told her to get a job, that she was a great solicitor, to stop waiting around for her life to start. He always knew when she needed some help.

The next bequest came from left field. Tommy was surprised, but had known that Ted had a soft spot for Cassie. He'd told Tommy what Cassie had done for Wendy and Ted when they were going through a rough patch when he was younger. Cassie was four years older than Tommy. Wendy had met her and taken her under her wing to sort out her family will - what Cassie didn't know was that it was Lizzie who had sorted it all out for her.

Mr Higgins coughed and said, "To the last bequest. 'I leave ten per cent of Tucker Builders Ltd to Cassie Davis, without whose help, giving me jobs to do, paying bills on time, finding friends who needed work done, and giving Ted's name to people who asked her if she could recommend a builder, at this time my business could have gone under. I am most heartedly grateful to her and I hope she never has a hard time in her life again.'"

Then Mr Higgins said, "'To my son Sam, I say this in the hope you won't feel hard done by: that at a time when you could have helped your family, you didn't. It was a good job I didn't say the same to you when you were at university, wanted a holiday or needed us to pay off your loan. It was your Mum and I who went without so that you could have the career you have now. I hope it makes you happy, I also hope that you too will look after your Mother and not leave it all to the others, and come to realise it's what you do to help others that counts, not what you do for yourself. I love you son. I hope you find some peace in your life. Dad.'"

There was silence.

Sam said, "How did you get my dad to give you ten per cent of the business? How?"

Wendy looked at him and said, "We've known Cassie for years. We met when you were at university and she has helped your Dad and me in tough times. Lizzie, this is the young girl I told you about. You sorted out her parents will, must be three or four years ago."

"Sam," Wendy said, "You know the rules. If you start anything today or any time after, you will have to return everything your father left you and hand it back to me."

Cassie sat in complete stock; Tommy lent in and asked if she was alright, stunned. she needed to talk to Wendy.

Lizzie suddenly stood and made an announcement. "I'm going back to work starting

Monday. I've got a really good job. Sam we need to talk, I know about your affairs. If you want this marriage to work, you're going to sell your flat. Things are going to change from *now*."

As she started to walked out of the room, she turned. "Cassie, I hope you and Tommy will be very happy, Ted loved you both so much."

She left with Sam running behind her.

The rest of this story is for another time.

The Mantra that Heals
Audrey

Some say it raises the vibrations
　Some that it changes brain chemistry
Others that it connects us to 'God'
　But I say: "Whatever! It works!"

Seems stupid to do it – who/what am I saying it to?
　Feels like the: "I love you" 30 x 4 times per day
I did in the 80s
　Words – and feelings about the words – so
dissonant
　I did not love me!

But (surprisingly) those words did change my
feelings
　How? I do not pretend to know
But the feelings went from dislike, through
neutral, to catching glimpses of a loveable person
　through to acceptance, and then, indeed, yes,
　to love.

Is it possible that this new mantra could/would
work?
　Say it deliberately – say it so often that it stays
Sounding in your unconscious – just say it!

I did.

And things <u>did</u> change:
   I saw people with new eyes, I saw The Past in
a new way
   I saw myself with a new compassion, and
      I saw my future looking "Orange"

The mantra that heals - past, present, and future -
      That triggers acceptance,
   That looks for the positive in tragedy,
      That sees the strength gained through adversity

I wish it had been hard to do – heroic even
      Its simplicity detracts from taking the idea
seriously
   Oh! What is it? This "mantra"?
   Two words:
      Thank You!

Lockdown Time
Bekhi Ostrowska

Lockdown begins, what do I find?

Time…

Time to be me. Time to be free.

I look out of the window and what do I see?

The wonders of my garden staring at me.

Two slabs lying flat on the ground.

My mind awakens. What have I found?

If I remove them and dig down deep,

A pond I can create for the frogs to sleep.

A place they can call home and catch their flies

Whilst being utter pleasure for my grandson's eyes.

Time…

Time to be me. Time to be free.

I stand in the garden and what do I behold?

Magnolia, Camellia, Cherry Blossom bold.

A place for the birds to build their nests

Whilst I sit beneath them and simply rest.

I sit and listen to the songs they make,

Sit and watch as the twigs they take

To line their nests for future life,

Safe from all troubles and strife.

Time…

Time to be me. Time to be free.

I sit under the fir tree and what do I spy?

A pile of branches and twigs catch my eye.

I wonder what I can do with these,

These branches salvaged from fallen trees.

I'll make a path. I'll weave and entwine

And at the end I'll display a sign,

"This is where creativity lives.

This is the treasure that lockdown gives."

Time.

About the Contributors

ADAM PARFITT moved to York at the age of 33 in 2012 to attend York St John University. He has been taken in many different directions to get where he is now, none of which he was expecting. He hopes that by sharing his sometimes dark experiences in his book, 'Aliens & Steam Irons', he has been able to convey the meaning of the life lessons he has experienced to his readers. Writing has certainly been helpful to him and if it had not been for the help of Emma McKenzie (Occupational Therapist) and the Converge team, Adam feels he would still feel lost. Thankfully, that is no longer the case; he can embrace who he is and look forward to what the future holds.

AMY STEWART is a freelance copywriter by day, writer of feminist, speculative fiction by night. She completed an MA in Creative Writing at York St John in 2019, graduating with a Distinction and the Programme Prize. Amy also received a Highly Commended Award in the 2019 Bridport Prize for her short story, *Wolf Women*. She's happiest on long walks in the Yorkshire countryside with her partner Phil and their rescue pup, Wolfie.

AUDREY. Once upon a time, in Bradford, there was a girl-child who knew she was a fairy. She danced on neighbours' lawns, one with sunshine, wind, birds and trees.

Fairies are not commonly thought to be curious but it is actually their core reality. Why can I hear the sea when I hang upside down? What sparkles in the sunbeam – diamond dust? Why, when I lie back on the roundabout, does it feel like I'm at the North Pole with the whole wide earth circling around me? How come, scraping at stone, I can make sand?
Fairies live in an enchanted world.

60 years later, the Crone sets out to re-enchant her world.

BRENDA HODGSON lives in York and has a Sociology degree from the Open University (2018). She enjoys creative writing and songwriting with Converge. Being part of these courses and the Communitas choir plus other courses such as Ecotherapy at St Nick's have helped her to recover from serious illness and loss. Highlights of her time with Converge have been visiting and recording at the Abbey Road studios in London with the Communitas choir and singing in the Minster in December for several years with the choir for the St John's University carol service.

CAROLINE lives in Yorkshire, her adopted home. This is her first foray into having her writing published. Maybe the first of many as there are a myriad of ideas and themes still to explore. Caroline is a dabbler, writing, reading and crafting is among the variety of activities she enjoys.

CATHERINE is a graduate in European studies with

French. She has an interest in art, music and creative writing and has completed courses in these subjects at Converge. Likes tea and cake.

CHARLEY lives in York with her wonderful dog Harry who just loves to play. Charley is a poet and abstract artist. She is inspired by York Art Gallery's collections and Harry. York Art Gallery is Charley's second home and she is always hanging out there enjoying the creative space and soaking up the inspiration. Adventures with Harry allow Charley to experience the joy of being alive and to find pleasure in the most simplest of things. She then translates her experiences into poetry and abstract painting. Charley also loves Lego and is creating her own Lego model railway!

CHRISTINA loves living in the North of England with her husband, and has found that writing has given her a new lease of life. She is finding her way by experimenting with different genres, which is giving her immense pleasure and expanding her knowledge. Christina loves walking, cooking, drawing and water colour painting.

ESTHER CLARE GRIFFITHS is a songwriter, mum and writer (not necessarily in that order!) She loves to write with her black Labrador snuggled up next to her – he's a great audience and is never quick to judge! In her memoirs, Esther writes of growing up in Northern Ireland, firm friends, long journeys in search of wine gums, and even a tin tub! She loves her work at Converge as Songwriting tutor and a leader of Communitas choir. Earlier this year she sang and co-wrote a song with musicians from York St John University and Communitas choir, which was recorded at Abbey Road Studios.

HELEN KENWRIGHT writes speculative and queer fiction, and teaches creative writing. She is Creative Writing Lead for Converge. Her publications include 'Women of White Water' in *Glass and Gardens: Solarpunk Summers*, 'Seeds of White Water' in *Terra Two: An Ark for Off-World Survival*, 'Smoke' in *Forest* and 'Drop in the Ocean' in *Ocean*. Her winning entry in the @SFFiction competition is published in *Serious Flash Fiction 4*.

She lives in York with two cats, and plays more video games than is seemly for a woman of her age.

HOLLY lives near York. She has dabbled in poetry and prose for over a decade. In her free time, you will find her drafting ideas for a future novel, surrounded by a growing number of unread books, hunting for inspiration. Holly is unable to form a coherent sentence without music, tea, and a spellchecker. Holly is a published author having also written for the first two anthologies.

JOANNE has always loved reading and has discovered through Converge an even greater love of writing. She has a particular leaning towards the dark and the absurd and is enjoying experimenting with different genres and themes.

Her only regret is that there are far too many wonderful things to read and write about, so many ideas to explore that she wishes she'd started far earlier!

JUNIOR MARK CRYLE was born and raised in the City of York, and lives with creativity as a self-certified dragon fanatic, from a love of illustrations to an interest in mythology. An optimist when it comes to fiction and life, he reflects this trait in his work as he takes pride in giving enjoyment to those around him. A silver tongue in conversation and a black belt in Karate, he is a force to be reckoned with.

KEITH is from North Yorkshire. He has done creative writing for a number of years. Some of it has been put into books for people to enjoy. He tries to rhyme his poetry but it's not always possible. He is classed as a mature student. He feels the help from Alex and Helen have given him has given him confidence to express his writing and do more poetry which he enjoys. He's also done a film and art course with Converge.

KAREN'S job with Converge is to support students to engage in learning. One of the perks of the role is to take part in Converge courses, and she has thoroughly enjoyed joining in with the Creative Writing course.

LOUISE RAW was born and lives in York. She has enjoyed writing for many years and has been published in community publications. She is currently writing a fantasy novella called The Cruellest Curse.

LYNNE PARKIN is a true Yorkshire Parkin. A fifty something female who lives with her husband, a

Bedlington terrier and a black cat. She is also a much loved grandma and behind her smile you will find a paperback serial killer who loves short stories, poetry and play writing.

LYKAELL DERT-ETHRAE was born in the suburbs of Aldvon on Covyn 5. She is currently one of the most prolific publishers on Ancient History for the Covyn Historical Society (CHS) and holds one of the chairs on their Board. Her best friend is renowned Project C, the only person in Covyn to publish more books on Ancient History than Lykaell. She currently resides in Lios where the headquarters of the CHS sits. Lykaell spends her free time running around like a little girl hugging trees and chasing cats as well as going off to exotic archaeological expeditions with her friend Project C.

MATT HARPER-HARDCASTLE is a theatre director, writer and tutor based in York. The Writing Tree published his debut book in 2019, *The Day The Alien Came;* a memoir of his mother's terminal illness, their collective journey through it and Matt's own relationship with grief.

MICHAEL lives somewhere around York. He did at one point have chickens as pets and still treats their disappearance as suspicious. He enjoys painting, drawing and sculpting when he can get peace and quiet.

ROSS is a relatively new author who made his debut with *Creative Writing Heals Volume Two*. His hobbies include reading, gaming and writing.

RUTH is Yorkshire born and returned to the county she loves in 2005 after time spent in London and the Midlands. An avid reader, Ruth has worked with the Ilkley Literature Festival as Fringe coordinator. She has also facilitated writing for well-being sessions with homeless people, people with head injuries, young people, including those in care. She is a trustee of, and volunteer with several health, arts, and LGBT organisations, nationally and locally. With a lifelong passion for tennis, Ruth is now finding herself to be quite a competitive but not a very competent boccia player!

SUE RICHARDSON lives in York with her husband and dog, Stan. Sue writes crime fiction and is fascinated by seemingly everyday characters who have a dark moral compass underneath. Hopefully she will show you everyone has a breaking point. *The Send-Off* is her debut piece.

WILLIAM writes short fiction mostly set in York, where he lives. He loves reading, especially the short stories of Lorrie Moore, Ali Smith and Sarah Hall.

About Converge

Converge is a partnership between York St John University and mental health service providers in the York region. It offers high quality educational opportunities to those who use NHS and non-statutory mental health services and who are 18 years and over.

Converge was established in 2008 from a simple idea: to offer good quality courses in a university setting to local people who use mental health services taught by students and staff. The development of Converge has progressively demonstrated the potential of offering educational opportunities to people who use mental health services, delivered by students and staff and held on a university campus. This has become the key principle which, today, remains at the heart of Converge. Born of a unique collaboration between the NHS and York St John University, Converge continues to deliver educational opportunities for people with mental health problems.

We offer work-based experience to university students involved in the programme. All classes are taught by undergraduate and postgraduate students, staff and, increasingly people who have lived experience of mental ill health. We have developed a solid track record of delivering quality courses. Careful support and mentoring underpin our work, thereby allowing students to experiment with their own ideas and creativity whilst gaining real world experience in the community. This undoubtedly enhances their employability in an increasingly competitive market.

As a leader in the field, Converge develops symbiotic projects and partnerships which are driven by innovation and best practice. The result is twofold: a rich and exciting educational opportunity for people with mental health problems alongside authentic and practical work experience for university students.

The aims of Converge are to:

- Work together as artists and students
- Build a community where we learn from each other
- Engage and enhance the university and wider community
- Provide a supportive and inclusive environment
- Respect others and value ourselves
- Above all, strive to be ordinary, extraordinary yet ourselves

About the Writing Tree

The Writing Tree is dedicated to the support and nurturing of creative writers. Founded in 2011, the Writing Tree offers one-to-one tuition, coaching and editing services and range of online and community courses.

The guiding principles of the Writing Tree are that creative writing has importance independent of subject, purpose or audience, and that everyone has the right to write, and to write what they wish.

The Writing Tree is honoured to publish 'Creative Writing Heals' for Converge. All proceeds from the book are donated to further the efforts of Converge writers.

You can find out more about the Writing Tree at www.writingtree.co.uk.

Just Write!

Whether you're a seasoned writer yourself or you've never picked up a pen before, you can start writing right now!

Pick a prompt from the list below, and start writing, set a timer for ten or twenty minutes, and freewrite - write without pausing, correcting or worrying about whether it's 'correct' or not. This is a great way to generate material for crafting into finished pieces later!

You can find more writing prompts and loads of advice and info about writing at our website:

https://convergeyorkcw.wordpress.com

Who knows – maybe this time next year your piece will be in 'Creative Writing Heals 4!'

Happy writing!

Prompts

1. There was something squeaking and it wasn't her sneakers.
2. It was a great day for swimming. Pity they were stuck in the desert…
3. He crept towards the cupboard and opened it to find….
4. Look out of the window and describe everything you see that has the colour white in it.
5. Think of a character (from books, film, TV or your own imagination). What would their favourite music playlist be?

Acknowledgements

Thank you to all our contributors, for having the courage to share their fantastic work.

Thank you to Paul Gowland for the fantastic cover image.

Thank you to all the Converge students, mentors, supporters and YSJ students for their help.

Thank you to Nick and Emma for guiding the Converge community through difficult waters in this pandemic year.

Thank you to all the staff at Converge for all they've done to support this production.

Thank you to the Igen Trust for resourcing and encouraging us.

And finally, thanks to our production team of Helen, Andy, Amy, Clare and William for being a magnificent crew for the tempestuous 2020 voyage of the Great Ship Overly Ambitious!

Printed in Poland
by Amazon Fulfillment
Poland Sp. z o.o., Wrocław

65448732R00106